———————————— ★ ————————————

No one was beside her. She was alone in the tunnel, flanked by dead bodies, and for a moment she could have sworn that one of them actually moved.

She was tempted to call out, but then she was afraid that someone would tell her to shut up, although that wouldn't be a bad thing because then she would know that someone else was in the building.

But of course someone else was in the building. What about that monk? And Father Felix was probably just around the corner.

Except that he wasn't. When she turned the corner and entered another room, all she saw were more dead bodies. She walked straight ahead, determined not to look left or right. And yet she had the distinct feeling that eyes were following her.

———————————— ★ ————————————

Previously published Worldwide Mystery title by
MARIANNA HEUSLER

MURDER AT ST. POLYCARP

CAPPUCCINO AT THE CRYPT
MARIANNA HEUSLER

W🌐RLDWIDE.

TORONTO • NEW YORK • LONDON
AMSTERDAM • PARIS • SYDNEY • HAMBURG
STOCKHOLM • ATHENS • TOKYO • MILAN
MADRID • WARSAW • BUDAPEST • AUCKLAND

Recycling programs
for this product may
not exist in your area.

CAPPUCCINO AT THE CRYPT

A Worldwide Mystery/April 2012

First published by Hilliard & Harris

ISBN-13: 978-0-373-63624-2

Copyright © 2011 by Marianna Heusler

Printed in U.S.A.

Dedicated to my dear sister-in-law,
Jamie Ramondetta, my first reader, in gratitude
for her constant support and encouragement.

udoran

ONE

SHE SHOULDN'T BE out this late—not here—and why couldn't he have agreed to meet her in a more public place? Her husband, Carlos, had never trusted him, but then again, Carlos hadn't trusted her much, either.

And just because Carlos was gone didn't mean that she shouldn't get what was coming to her. She knew where it was—but she needed help.

Besides, it was just a matter of time before it all came crashing down. Carlos had told her that he had gone to confession. He wasn't worried because priests are bound by the seal of the confessional. As long as the sinner is alive.

Only now the sinner was dead.

She turned down the darkened street and almost tripped over a lump at her feet. At first she thought it was just another beggar, an old man who might at any moment spring up and start screaming at her in a Sicilian dialect.

There was no way around it, though. She would just have to walk on by. She caught movement out of the corner of her eye and then she breathed a sigh of relief.

It was just another malnourished dog, a little brown and white mutt. She couldn't even bear to look into its pleading eyes, begging for food, for water, for love, for a home.

She glanced away and, from above, a stone gargoyle grimaced down at her. For a moment she thought he might fall and crash on her head.

She stepped off the narrow cobblestones and into the main road at the same time a motorcycle sped by, missing her by mere inches. She held her handbag against her ribs. She knew that the driver may try to grab it as had happened yesterday.

She slipped into the shelter of the shadowy alleyway. Was this the right place? In Palermo it was hard to tell. All alleys looked alike, an entanglement of small, irregular squares, black and narrow walkways, leading to dark stone structures.

No, she was in the right place. Above her a string of laundry—a tablecloth, a beige shirt, two pairs of old lady panties blew in the breeze. And a bright red blanket flapped angrily.

She took a few steps and then looked around.

The alley was completely deserted.

Please God, she thought, *don't let him be late.* Although thinking about the meeting sent a chill through her, a chill that had nothing to do with the April weather.

Somewhere in the distance a flock of geese squealed and then there was silence.

Someone was coming. She heard the sound of heels in back of her, clacking on the stones. But there was a twist in the path, so she couldn't see, not really.

She didn't dare go to investigate. Instead she glanced at a wooden door in front of her, probably locked.

A shadow magnified on the stone wall. It was probably him, a tall man. Except why was he dressed like a monk—and why was he swinging that rope belt?

Something was reaching for her throat.

Her first thought was that she was having some sort of nightmare. But that didn't stop her from turning around and running towards the street as fast as her ballet slippers would allow.

And why hadn't she stayed in America—with her family, where she would have been safe from all this madness?

She was going to be punished—she had no right to be here. Her breath came in gasps as she flew out of the darkened street, wondering who would come to her aid at this time of night.

She was in the middle of the road when she

heard it, the whizzing of a motorcycle, screeching down the street with a deafening sound, and he couldn't have stopped even if he wanted to, even if he saw her in the pitch-black darkness where just one old-fashioned bulb lit the area.

She felt an indescribable pain in her groin as her right leg ripped from her torso and then she fell backward when her head hit the concrete. It happened in a manner of seconds but it seemed as though she lay there forever, not feeling anything below the waist, drenched in wet, shocking, scarlet blood, her vision blurry, her nausea rising…the very last thing she saw as she lay dying in Sicily was the monk coming towards her holding that frayed piece of rope.

TWO

"WHAT ARE YOU DOING?" Amelia Johnston asked crisply.

"You mean now? At this precise moment?" Julia Hopwood answered on the other end of the telephone. She didn't dare tell Mrs. Johnston that she was in the middle of watching a Lifetime movie. Mrs. Johnston had no patience for television or movies, Lifetime or otherwise, since her own life was far more dramatic than any fiction on television.

Luckily, she had no patience for lulls in the conversation, either. "I have a question for you. Actually, it's a job offer."

"We have jobs, remember? I teach second grade at St. Polycarp and you teach seventh grade. And summer vacation is a mere two weeks away."

"It's a summer job."

Mrs. Hopwood did not have to think twice. One of the main reasons she chose teaching as a profession was for the summer vacations, so she could sleep late (or at least as late as her husband and son and dog would allow), so she could perfect her brownie recipe, so she could lunch with her friends, and watch movies, and read romance books… "I'm not teaching summer school." She made her voice sound firm because Mrs. Johnston had a way of talking her into things she didn't want to do.

"Who said anything about teaching summer school?"

Mrs. Hopwood paused for a moment and then said quickly, "I need some time to myself."

"It wouldn't be for long."

Mrs. Hopwood was not about to be persuaded. "Remember the other job you talked me into? That horrible development job when we had to stay after school and you told me it would just be for a few hours and it turned out to be every day after school until six o'clock and we had to fight Father Felix for the money, which he almost demanded back, when the banner you chose fell off the pole…"

"I chose?"

"I told you that we should have gone with the lightweight one. And then it fell on Thalia Thompson and gave her such a bump and Mr. Thompson wanted to sue Father Felix…"

"He's doing it."

"Who? Mr. Thompson?"

"No. Father Felix. He's taking the job."

"I'm not."

"Will you stop interrupting and just please listen? It's only for a week. And it pays five hundred dollars."

"Five hundred dollars for a week isn't very much money." Still there was that Macy's bill that Mr. Hopwood did not know about and the Sears credit card payment which was overdue.

"And a trip to Palermo." There was a hint of boosting in her tone.

For a moment Mrs. Hopwood thought she might have heard wrong, especially since her son, Alex, was blasting his music so loudly.

"Palermo, Sicily," Mrs. Johnston said, "and don't you have Sicilian relatives?"

"On my mother's side."

"Well, there you go," she said brusquely.

"Where am I going?"

"To Sicily. With me and Father Felix. We'll be traveling as chaperones with twenty-five girls from St. Hilda's High School and you know how lovely the girls are there. All we have to do is make sure that none of them falls off a cliff or gets hit in the head with an ancient stone."

"I hate teenagers," Mrs. Hopwood grumbled.

"But I've just explained to you, that these are nice teenagers and they're all girls. Our expenses will be paid and we'll be staying in a first-class hotel."

"That's what Father Felix told me when he talked me into going on that horrid trip for the Educational Evaluation and the first-class hotel turned out to be a drafty retreat house with mashed peas for supper."

"That was after Miss Pinkerton died."

"Was murdered," Mrs. Hopwood corrected.

"And everything was upside down. This is entirely different, a wonderful opportunity."

Mrs. Hopwood felt herself weakening so she responded with a great deal of irritation. "How did you find out about this, anyway?"

"Father Felix actually found the trip and offered it to me with the hopes that I would offer it to you."

"And he didn't have the nerve to ask me himself," Mrs. Hopwood said dryly.

"So are you in or not?"

"I have to discuss it with my husband. It's not like I can just leave my family and go abroad."

"Oh please!" Mrs. Johnston moaned. "If I can leave my four-year-old twin boys, and you know what a terror they are, with my mother and my husband, and you know how helpless he is, and he can manage on his own, I would think that your family can fend for themselves. I'll sign you up."

Abruptly Mrs. Johnston disconnected before Mrs. Hopwood had a chance to argue some more or even to ask when she'd have to make this trip and did she have time to get a passport. It didn't matter. The music coming from Alex's room was earsplitting and, when she stepped into the hall, she realized why.

The stereo was on, as were his television and his computer. "Turn that sound down!" she screamed at the top of her lungs.

"I have to hear it," he said sullenly.

"They can hear it in Russia."

He turned the volume down on the television, but did nothing to the stereo or the computer.

"I think you should know," she stood on the threshold of his room, "that I'm leaving town."

Alex did not even look up.

"I am leaving the country for Palermo."

"Where's that?"

"In Sicily."

Alex merely shrugged as he clicked the keys on his computer.

"And," Mrs. Hopwood threatened, "I have a good mind not to come back."

THREE

FATHER FELIX SAT at his desk and looked over the itinerary. They would visit Agrigento, an archeological site; Cefalu, the seaside town; medieval Erice; and the Nebrodi Mountains. Segesta, Taormina and Marsala were also listed on the tour as well as the small fishing village of Sferracavallo. Twenty-five giggling girls on the top of the mountain, pushing and screaming as they advanced towards the ocean. Already, he had a headache.

But it was the only way he could go to Sicily without looking suspicious. And dragging Mrs. Johnston and Mrs. Hopwood along was a brilliant idea—it made the whole thing seem more natural, more real. And, as much as he hated to admit it, he took a certain comfort in their dramatic personalities.

There was something he had to find, something he had to make right. The problem, though, nagged at his conscience. What he was about to do was quite dangerous and to expose twenty-five innocent girls to peril was hardly fair.

Well, Mrs. Hopwood and Mrs. Johnston would keep them safe. Maybe.

He would have to take care of his business while they were taking care of the girls and keep as many secrets from them as he could. He would have to distract them and insist upon free time to himself. And hope that God would protect him.

FOUR

"Do you have your passport?" Mrs. Johnston asked Mrs. Hopwood. She was squished in the back of a car with Father Felix on one side and Mrs. Hopwood on the other and a sulky driver in front.

"I do."

"And your plane ticket?"

"I do."

"Remember you can't bring any liquids on the plane, or tweezers, or scissors," Mrs. Johnston continued in a condescending tone.

"I have been on a plane before, Amelia."

"It's only that if you don't have everything you need, we should turn back right away because you can't get on the plane without…"

"We can't turn back," the driver said heatedly. "You see that traffic up ahead. That's the Lincoln Tunnel. As it is, it will take us at least an hour before we hit Newark Airport. We got no time to turn back."

"We got no time to turn back." Mrs. Hopwood

repeated as she fussily checked the clasp of her oversize handbag.

"The girls will be meeting us in the waiting area," Father Felix said as the car swerved and he fell into Mrs. Johnston who squealed. "Who has the list?"

Mrs. Johnston stared at Mrs. Hopwood, whom she had been foolish enough to entrust the list to.

"Me." Mrs. Hopwood straightened up.

"May I see it?" Father Felix asked politely.

Mrs. Hopwood looked confused.

"What's the matter?" Mrs. Johnston could see that this wasn't going to be an easy trip and staying home with her twin boys and her husband began to look better.

"It's in my overnight case, which is on the floor."

"So get it," Father Felix demanded.

Mrs. Hopwood shrugged and attempted to reach for her orange bag, which was almost as large as the suitcase Mrs. Johnston brought for the entire trip. Mrs. Hopwood sat the bag on her lap, where it spilled onto Mrs. Johnston's lap, which forced her to move closer to Father Felix, who leaned against the window.

Mrs. Hopwood unzipped her bag and proceeded to rifle through it, tossing clothes on the floor.

Mrs. Johnston stared in disbelief as she caught a

glimpse of what was coming out of the bag, sparkling, strapless tops, pencil skirts, chiffon dresses and high-heel sandals.

"Where do you think you're going?" Father Felix grimaced.

"What do you mean? I'm going to Palermo, where you said it was going to be warm."

"You look like you're going to a cocktail party," Mrs. Johnston said. "You can't possibly wear all that clothing. We are responsible for twenty-five impressionable teenagers."

"I don't know how impressionable they are." Mrs. Hopwood had now reached the bottom of the bag and a pink and red polka dot thong landed on Father Felix's lap, where he leaned back, aghast.

"Tell her that she can't wear those clothes," Mrs. Johnston said, turning toward Father Felix who had leaned back in horror, trying to escape from the thong. "Oh my God—I can't believe you brought those yellow shoes. Are you out of your mind?" She gasped.

For a moment Mrs. Hopwood appeared as though she were seriously considering the question.

Mrs. Johnston continued. "What sort of a trip do you think this is? Those heels have to be at least five inches high."

"No, let me show you something." Mrs. Hopwood reached for the heel and began to unscrew it, thereby bumping into Father Felix who uttered an audible huff. "Could you ladies do this show-and-tell somewhere else—like maybe in your hotel room?"

"This is important," Mrs. Hopwood insisted stubbornly. "Look, the heel comes off."

"So what does that mean," Mrs. Johnston asked. "Now you not only have a hideous shoe, but a broken shoe."

"No great loss," Father Felix mumbled as she shifted in his seat.

"Not broken at all," Mrs. Hopwood said cheerfully and she began to dig into her purse.

"Please stop bumping me," Father Felix pleaded.

"Okay, I'll just tell you," Mrs. Hopwood said. "In my purse, there is a kitten heel so you see I can change the heel height at will. Isn't that clever? And they weigh practically nothing because the heels are hollow."

"Someone could use it for smuggling." Mrs. Johnston had had enough. "Although I doubt you'll be wearing those shoes period. Now could you please move your overnight bag? It's hitting me in the stomach and I think I'm going to vomit."

Mrs. Hopwood threw the shoes in her bag and then exclaimed, "Here it is! This is what I was looking for." Mrs. Hopwood took out a brochure with a skeleton on the cover.

Mrs. Johnston was horrified. "The names of the girls are in there?"

"No. This is something Alex gave me. It's a place we simply must visit. The Capuchin Catacombs. Eight thousand bodies are hanging there, well, some of them are just in open coffins. They have been embalmed in vinegar, except sometimes it didn't work so well, so they're half skeleton but with some skin still intact, like an ear or a hand..."

"That's not on our tour," Mrs. Johnston said somewhat tartly.

"I know but we do have some leisure time and I think the girls..."

"I think," Father Felix said loudly in a tone of righteous authority, "that you should find the list and stop all of this nonsense."

Mrs. Johnston agreed wholeheartedly with Father Felix's reprimand, but she resented it, nevertheless. She knew now that he was going to be irritable and bossy, probably for the duration of the trip. While she didn't mind taking orders from him (well, maybe she did mind a little bit) when she was teaching (after all he was the principal, he had hired her and probably had the power to fire her), they were not in school now and he had no more authority over her and Mrs. Hopwood than she had over him. And sooner or later, she was afraid that her temper would snap and she would say something she might regret, which would make the entire trip miserable as well as jeopardize her job in the fall.

"Here it is." Mrs. Hopwood held a very wrinkled piece of paper in her hand. "The girls all have very odd names, Summer, Dior, Sapphire, Ruby, Pearl…"

"What are we taking, a jewelry box?" Mrs. Johnston asked. Mrs. Hopwood was still holding the paper but Father Felix seemed to have lost interest in it. Instead he was staring at the brochure about the catacombs with a rather grim expression. He had gone pale and Mrs. Johnston was afraid that he was going to be ill. On her lap.

"Are you okay?"

"I'm fine," Mrs. Hopwood said airily. "Although how I'm going to get all this stuff back into my carry-on."

"I wasn't talking to you."

"And you have some nerve criticizing my wardrobe. That fanny pack you're wearing is beyond ugly. No one wears fanny packs anymore. They are totally out of style. Isn't that true?" She turned toward Father Felix.

"I don't know." He shrugged. "I have one."

"Well, you're a man. And a priest. So you can get away with wearing ugly things."

"I don't care," Mrs. Johnston patted hers. "At least it's not a neon color. And it holds my passport, my cell phone and my wallet. I dare anyone to try and rob me with it so close to my heart."

"You mean close to your groin," Mrs. Hopwood corrected her friend.

Suddenly Father Felix grabbed the list, reaching over Mrs. Johnston and pulling her forward as the car took a nasty lurch. He mumbled something under his breath.

Mrs. Johnston was feeling very nauseous and they weren't even on the plane yet.

FIVE

SAPPHIRE SULLIVAN LEANED BACK in her seat, heart-sick as she listened to the laughter and the excitement of twenty-four girls. Her stomach felt jumpy and funny and all she could hope was that she wasn't going to be sick, right here on the bus. If she was feeling this way now, what would it be like on the eight-hour plane ride, or on the tour bus rattling over all those bumpy village roads?

Just take it one day at a time, she reminded herself

"I wonder if we're going to be able to go to any clubs."

"I'm going—if I have to sneak out."

"Maybe I'll meet some Mafia boys—like on *The Sopranos*."

"Oh—they are so sexy."

She opened her eyes and looked out the window. Her final glance at Manhattan made her glad she was leaving. All the traffic and the horns and the people rushing around, all of them thinking they were so important, that they were on their way to something that mattered.

As though anything mattered.

I'm going to be all right, she told herself, even though she knew it was a lie. At least for a little while, I'm going to be all right.

She tried not to think about her mother, when she kissed her good-bye. It was her seven-year-old sister she would miss the most. Chloe was so sweet and kind, so generous and unspoiled. She deserved a better mother, a better world. And what would happen to her now?

Can't think about that, she told herself, as she blinked back the tears. I'm doing what I have to do. She took one fleeting look at Manhattan as they entered the Lincoln Tunnel and wondered if she'd be coming back.

SIX

"I DON'T THINK IT'S RIGHT," Mrs. Johnston complained to Mrs. Hopwood as they headed towards Gate B43.

Mrs. Hopwood didn't respond. She was just relieved that her luggage, although it exceeded the fifty-pound limit by thirteen pounds, had been whisked away, and she felt strangely free and lighthearted. Now she just had to lug around this orange carry-on case and maybe Mrs. Johnston was right, she had packed too many things, but how was she supposed to know when she never went anyplace?

"The way he broke up the girls, I mean."

Mrs. Hopwood was tempted to put down her carry-on and take a breather but Mrs. Johnston, who was in a snit about something or other, was walking much too fast and besides, Mrs. Hopwood didn't want to give her friend the satisfaction of knowing she was right about the excess baggage.

"You know, that we each had to be responsible for nine girls."

"That seems reasonable to me."

"It's totally unreasonable," Mrs. Johnston snapped angrily. "He made sure he only has seven! And what if the nine girls I'm responsible for aren't even friends and what if they don't want to hang around with each other and want to break up and go with other people? I mean, shouldn't we have let the girls decide? They might be unhappy and unhappy teenagers can make you miserable."

Mrs. Hopwood knew all about unhappy teenagers, thanks to her son. But right now she was envying Mrs. Johnston with her little tote bag, which she carried with ease, on her shoulder.

"I have to go to the bathroom," Mrs. Hopwood said suddenly as she staggered and stumbled.

"Didn't you go before you left home?" There was a tinge of impatience in Mrs. Johnston's voice, as though she were speaking to one of her seventh grade students.

"It's all that coffee I've been drinking," she answered in a great heaving breath.

"Oh, I can see, you're going to be a joy on the plane."

"Which is why I can't have a window seat," Mrs. Hopwood reminded her, "that and the fact that I'm claustrophobic."

"Just hurry up. Father Felix is probably waiting for us and he's going to be very crabby if he has to deal with twenty-five teenage girls on his own."

Mrs. Hopwood lugged her carry-on to the restroom, huffing and puffing. She really didn't have to go to the bathroom. What she needed to do was rest a bit. Unlike Mrs. Johnston who was fit and strong, Mrs. Hopwood was not used to carrying around a set of twins and hauling this bag was a struggle. Once inside, though, she decided she might as well go into the bathroom, because, if Mrs. Johnston was going to complain every time she had to visit the toilet, well, it wasn't going to be easy for her, either. They said you never knew people until you traveled with them.

All the stalls were empty except one but Mrs. Hopwood chose the first because she had read somewhere that was usually the cleanest, since everyone avoided it because they expected it to be the dirtiest.

She was busy trying to put down her luggage when she heard the sound of sobs. Someone was wailing and Mrs. Hopwood was curious. She wanted to get out of the cubicle to see who the crier was. So she finished what she had to do quickly and, just as she was exiting the stall, she heard the unmistakable sound of vomiting coming from the closed door.

Mrs. Hopwood was no longer curious.

She hurried to the sink and washed her hands, while the heaving continued. Just as she was looking for the paper towels (before discovering that there were none) the vomiter emerged. A young, pretty girl stumbled over to the sink. She briefly examined her pale face in the mirror. Her blonde ponytail was coming apart, her lip gloss was smudged and her white sweatshirt was stained, her jeans a little too large. She didn't even glance in Mrs. Hopwood's direction.

Mrs. Hopwood bent down to get her own carry-on, when she noticed the girl's tote bag on the floor. It had a bright pink tag on it, much like the bright pink tag on her own luggage. And then Mrs. Hopwood knew that this girl was probably part of the tour and probably pregnant and probably in Mrs. Hopwood's group and she wasn't feeling happy about this at all.

She picked up her own suitcase, only it seemed heavier than it had before, so the respite only made it more difficult to continue.

"What took you so long?" Mrs. Johnston demanded, a little nettled.

"There was a girl in there, throwing up."

"So?"

"She's in our group. I saw the pink tag."

Mrs. Johnston's only response was a huff. "And I suppose you were talking to her, giving her all sorts of advice, and you knew that I was waiting for you and Father Felix is waiting for us."

Mrs. Hopwood walked several steps behind Mrs. Johnston, who made no attempt to wait for her as she hurried towards the gate.

Mrs. Hopwood was longing for an ice-cold glass of water, and maybe a bite to eat, and she was tempted to dump her carry-on right then and there, and she was wishing with all her heart that she had stayed home.

SEVEN

FATHER FELIX STOPPED at a Starbucks, ordered himself a latte and took a chair facing the wall. He didn't want to see Mrs. Johnston or Mrs. Hopwood and more importantly, he didn't want them to see him.

He didn't want them to see him shaking.

He couldn't tell a soul what he was about to do, not if he respected the bounds of confession. And he couldn't put anyone, not the teachers, and certainly not the students in danger. He would have to do this all on his own, although how he was to manage was beyond him.

He heard them before he saw them. Mrs. Hopwood, luggage laden and whining and Mrs. Johnston reprimanding her. This was going to be some trip. Then he heard Mrs. Hopwood insist on stopping for coffee.

"We don't have time," Mrs. Johnston said decisively. "The girls are waiting at the gate!"

"You go and I'll get you something."

"Well."

"A sandwich, too, if you want or a brownie and a cappuccino."

Mrs. Johnston appeared to be thinking about it. Father Felix didn't dare look. But it didn't matter because a moment later he heard Mrs. Hopwood bellow, "Oh guess who's here!"

And then he heard the patter of high-heel shoes in his direction.

"There you are!" she said as he turned around and watched Mrs. Johnston disappear from view. After a few faltering steps, Mrs. Hopwood, breathless and panting, collapsed in the chair beside him and dropped her bright orange tote bag where it clanged on the floor.

"What do you have in there?" he grumbled. "And what makes you think they're going to let you take all of that on the plane?"

"Please, don't ask." Her face darkened with indignation. "I've already been lectured by Amelia. Do you think you could watch it while I get something for her to eat? She can't go too long you know without something sweet." She rose and then sank down again. "You will go to the crypts with me," she said suddenly, "won't you?"

The way she asked, coming to him that way, he wondered if she could have guessed. But no, there was no way she could have put it together. If it had been Mrs. Johnston, he might have thought she suspected something, but Mrs. Hopwood was not suspicious by nature. She was rather naive and that might serve him well.

"It's not on the tour," he managed to sound irritable, "but we do have some leisure time so maybe we could take a look. I know that Mrs. Johnston isn't interested."

'She's determined to go to the flea market and come back with some Sicilian toys for her twins."

Father Felix took a gulp of his coffee, which had turned cold. "We'll see." He stood, thinking it would be better not to commit himself. "We might as well wait with the girls. We really don't have time to order coffee and brownies—just look at the line." He knew Mrs. Hopwood was not a patient woman.

He rose slowly and watched her grimace as she lifted her suitcase.

"Here give me that!" He took it from her and almost stumbled from the weight. "What do you have in here?" he asked for the second time.

She only shrugged.

Clothes, he was betting, all sorts of crazy outfits with matching shoes and bags and accessories. He doubted very much if she would be able to wear them all, but knowing Mrs. Hopwood, she probably would. Straight into the crypt.

EIGHT

SAPPHIRE'S HEART BEAT fast and furiously. Act natural, she told herself, there is no way that they're going to stop you. Not a Catholic school girl, traveling with Catholic school teachers on a Catholic tour with a Catholic priest.

Still she didn't feel good. Not after meeting that teacher and Sapphire knew that she was a teacher right away. Not that she looked like one. What she looked like was an ordinary lady, trying to be Jennifer Lopez. She was wearing a bright red dress above her knees (and her legs were flabby, too) and a ton of bronzer and scarlet lipstick. Then there was all that jewelry, lots of bangle bracelets and big hoop earrings and that ridiculous necklace with a gold flower in the middle.

It was the orange overnight bag which gave her away. It had her initials on it and Sapphire knew that the woman must have ordered it from one of those mail-order catalogs that teachers love. Plus, she had a canvas pocketbook with a pad in it and a bottle of water (like she planned on doing a lot of talking) and then a bag of Hershey Kisses like every teacher gives kids to get them to shut up.

At least the kids not allergic to nuts.

Sapphire was real observant, as smart as a whip. So how come she was doing something so dumb? She needed the money, and not to buy souvenirs, like fancy Italian handbags, eighteen-karet gold necklaces but money to plan her escape. What did these girls know? How could they possibly understand what Sapphire was going through? If her father had lived—if on that March morning, when the world was alive and bursting with the promise of spring, his heart hadn't stopped beating—if he hadn't left her mother penniless, then maybe her mother wouldn't have married Bruce. And maybe if Bruce hadn't hit her mother—maybe her mother wouldn't have started drinking.

If Sapphire could just get a little money, she'd hop on a Peter Pan bus and take her little sister far away to Iowa, where she had cousins, where her sister would be safe. Because it was only a matter of time before Bruce started on her. I'm going to be all right…Sapphire repeated to herself like a mantra…I'm going to be all right.

NINE

Mrs. Hopwood was claustrophobic so she could not be squished in the middle of the three seats. She also suffered from dizziness so she could not sit by a window. She had to be placed near the aisle. Which meant Father Felix sat by the window and Mrs. Johnston (who was easily the biggest of the three) was in between. Mrs. Johnston might not have minded that so much if Mrs. Hopwood didn't have so much stuff.

Her overnight bag did not fit in the compartment above (which was no surprise to anyone). Instead it had to be placed under her seat (and partially under Mrs. Johnston's). Her blanket was also on the floor draped over Mrs. Johnston's shoes. Scattered below were magazines about the lives of the rich and famous and the young and stupid. On Mrs. Hopwood's seat was a bag of Hershey Kisses, a box of chocolate chip cookies (which she had purchased duty-free and saved a total of six cents) and a sequined sweater, whose glitter was coming off and falling on Mrs. Johnston's very sensible shoes.

To make matters worse Father Felix was sound asleep, snoring with gusto, his mouth open, his head leaning on Mrs. Johnston's shoulder.

Mrs. Johnston tried desperately to snooze. She was just dozing off, when she felt a poke in the ribs and her eyes flew open. "What?" she asked impatiently.

"How is this pillow supposed to go?" Mrs. Hopwood complained. "Is it supposed to be under your back or cradling your neck?"

"It's supposed to be under your neck," Mrs. Johnston answered irritably. "Please! I'm trying to sleep. It's two in the morning, USA time."

"It's nine in the morning Sicily time," Mrs. Hopwood said cheerfully.

"I'm still in the USA!" Mrs. Johnston snapped.

Mrs. Hopwood was quiet—for a moment.

"You see that girl over there," she asked suddenly.

"There are a lot of girls over there."

"The one in blue. That's the one who threw up in the bathroom."

"Maybe she's scared of planes."

"I told you she was crying, too."

"So maybe she's homesick."

"Her name is Sapphire Sullivan. Remember? She's in your group."

"Okay." Mrs. Johnston adjusted her own neck pillow and closed her eyes.

"She might be pregnant."

"Listen." Mrs. Johnston's head popped up which sent Mrs. Hopwood's plastic glass of water flying, mostly on Mrs. Johnston's lap. "I don't care. I don't care if she's sick, I don't care if she's sad. I am only in charge of her for seven days. Now I want to go to sleep!"

Father Felix's eyes snapped open and he shot them a withering look. "What's all the screaming?"

Mrs. Johnston stared at him. "You were snoring and keeping the entire plane up."

He glared at her and then announced that he was going to the bathroom.

That meant that Mrs. Hopwood had to move first, which she did with a great deal of confusion. Her pillow went flying, she stepped over magazines, and her bag of Hershey Kisses tumbled into the aisle.

Mrs. Johnston managed to rise with some dignity but then she thought just how sloppy Mrs. Hopwood was. It was one thing to visit her untidy classroom. It would be another matter entirely to share a hotel room with her.

Mrs. Hopwood was picking candy off the floor,

trying to physically grab it from a toddler, when Mrs. Johnston noticed it.

Something was sticking out of the pocket of Father Felix's backpack. It was a picture of the crypts and she doubted very much it was the same brochure that Mrs. Hopwood had shown him.

Carefully she removed the paper and noticed that it was stapled with a map of Palermo. Clearly he had brought this with him, so why had he acted so surprised when Mrs. Hopwood mentioned the crypts, like he had never heard of them before? There were also some notes on the paper and luckily Father Felix had impeccable handwriting. If these papers had belonged to Mrs. Hopwood, Mrs. Johnston would be out of luck.

Room for the priests. Body number #772? Massive head wound. Blue robe. Hook for hand.

Mrs. Johnston stared at the piece of paper. It might have well been written by Mrs. Hopwood for all the sense it made to her.

Mrs. Hopwood collapsed in the seat, her mouth bulging with chocolate. She offered some Kisses to Mrs. Johnston, who would have snatched them up except some of the silver foil was torn and God only knew where they had been.

"What's that?" Mrs. Hopwood had seen the brochure.

Mrs. Johnston stuffed it back into Father Felix's backpack.

"Something is going on with him," she whispered impressively, "and it has to do with the dead bodies." Mrs. Johnston put her fingers to her lips, the way Mrs. Hopwood did to her second graders. Mrs. Johnston, on the other hand, merely told her seven graders to shut up.

Mrs. Hopwood did shut up, at least for the moment. She whipped her head around and pointed to the steward who was rolling a cart down the aisle, blocking Father Felix.

Mrs. Johnston intended to find out what secret Father Felix was harboring, because, after all, she was responsible for nine girls and herself and her two twin boys who were counting on her to come home in one piece.

TEN

Mrs. Hopwood couldn't sleep. For one thing Mrs. Johnston not only snored, she talked in her sleep. She screamed at her students, yelled at her twin boys and argued with her husband.

For another thing it was so blasted hot in the room. She was drenched in sweat. Didn't Sicilians believe in air-conditioning? Or were they just immune after generations of heat?

Mrs. Johnston had grabbed the window by the bed. She just plopped her suitcase there without a discussion and began to unpack, choosing the first two drawers in the dresser and the right side of the closet. She also hogged most of the bathroom shelf with all of her creams and hair products.

Mrs. Hopwood couldn't take it anymore. She threw off the sheet and jumped out of bed. She tiptoed over to the window, squeezing her body between Mrs. Johnston's bed and the wall. She found the latch and it squeaked loudly as she attempted to turn it.

Like she was being shot from a cannon, Mrs.

Johnston bolted upright in her bed. "What are you doing?" she screamed.

"I have to have some air. I feel as though I'm going to faint."

"You have kept me up all night," Mrs. Johnston said heatedly, "tossing and turning. I haven't slept a wink."

Mrs. Hopwood couldn't think of a quick retort to this absurd statement, so she just flung open the window.

"I don't think that's a good idea," Mrs. Johnston said. "In case you haven't noticed, there are no screens. All sorts of foreign bugs can fly in here, bugs that we have not been inoculated from."

Somewhere in the distance a gaggle of geese honked. "That's probably our supper tomorrow night," Mrs. Hopwood said. So far she was not pleased with Sicilian food. Tonight they had eaten at the hotel, pasta with broccoli. Broccoli gave her awful gas. Then a veal chop, and Mrs. Hopwood refused to eat veal because of the way they mistreated the animals. For dessert there was some sort of ice cream. Mrs. Hopwood was lactose intolerant.

Mrs. Johnston, on the other hand, not only gobbled her own food down, but Mrs. Hopwood's as well, because as she explained, "it was already paid for."

"Close that window and come to bed!" Mrs. Johnston ordered.

But Mrs. Hopwood spotted a familiar figure emerging from the shadows below.

"Amelia, come over here, quickly."

Mrs. Johnston's reply was to throw the covers over her head.

"I am begging you."

"I don't want to see any geese. I did not travel thousands of miles to see geese."

"It's not a goose, it's a girl."

"I did not travel thousands of miles to see a girl. I see plenty of girls in my own classroom."

"It's not just any girl. It's Sapphire." Sapphire was leaning against the wall, smoking a cigarette, dressed in black. "And she's smoking and she's pregnant."

"You don't know that she's pregnant."

"That's true. But she looks as if she's waiting for someone. She's alone in the dark in a foreign country and you're responsible for her because, after all, she's on your list."

Mrs. Johnston threw off her tangled sheets. "I can't help it if some girl takes it in her head to sneak out to meet someone in the middle of the night. Maybe she likes an Italian waiter or the bus driver. If you hadn't picked this precise moment to look out the window, we wouldn't even know what she was doing."

"But because we do know, aren't we responsible?"

Mrs. Johnston pushed Mrs. Hopwood aside, stuck her full face out the window and opened her mouth.

"What are you doing?" Mrs. Hopwood yanked on the tail of her nightgown.

"I'm going to yell down to her and tell her to go back to the hotel and climb into bed."

"That won't solve anything."

"In case you don't remember," Mrs. Johnston said wearily, "tomorrow we have a full day. We're going to the Oratorio del Rosario first thing in the morning. I don't want to solve any problems. What I want to do is get some sleep."

"We have a responsibility." From the look on Mrs. Johnston's face, it was apparent that she didn't care about responsibility, so Mrs. Hopwood decided to appeal to a much stronger emotion. "We have to see what she's up to. For all we know she's waiting for an abortionist. If she should bleed to death…"

Just then Mrs. Hopwood got a terrible thought. What if while she was arguing with Mrs. Johnston, Sapphire had already left?

She glanced out the window. Sapphire was still

there, but she had finished her cigarette and she was now glancing at her watch impatiently.

Mrs. Johnston sat on the bed. "I know," her voice was filled with skepticism, "that I'm going to hate myself in the morning for asking this question, but what exactly do you expect us to do?"

"Follow her, of course," Mrs. Hopwood said simply.

"I've got to tell you," Mrs. Johnston searched under the bed for her walking shoes, "My heart is just not in this."

"It's not your heart we need so much. It's your legs."

ELEVEN

SHE SHOULDN'T BE SMOKING. She knew that. Not that she was worried about the negative effects on her long-term health. She didn't expect to live that long. She was concerned because someone might see the lit cigarette in the dark.

From several stories above she heard two people arguing.

Where was he? He had said that he would meet her in this alley at two-thirty and it was after that now. Shouldn't he be on time? Weren't these people always on time?

Obviously not.

In the corner Sapphire saw something on the ground. Cautiously, she crept over and picked it up. It was cheap plastic compact—engraved with the words— "I can face anything if I'm wearing the right shoes."

Sapphire was wearing sneakers.

For some reason she thought about the over-dressed chaperone, who always seemed to have on the wrong kind of shoes, only maybe the chaperone thought they were the right kind of shoes.

Sapphire flipped open the compact expecting to see the shadow of her puffy, tired face staring back at her. Instead she found a tiny, piece of paper folded up.

Her heart pounding, she opened it. A number in red had been scrawled—#772.

She folded up the paper again and put it in her jean pocket and tossed the compact.

She heard a noise and the door creaked open.

She stepped further into the shadows.

The door continued to open. From where she was standing she couldn't see much. Except that he wasn't him. Instead she saw a round cocoa-colored face which she recognized as belonging to the African-American chaperone. And behind her was that flighty teacher, dressed in a Kelly green jogging suit.

Sapphire wondered what they were doing out here in the middle of the night. And then she knew that somehow they had been spying on her but they were too stupid to realize that if you were going to do something that sneaky, you should at least have the good sense to wear a dark color.

If he came, she was dead meat.

She turned around and saw that the alley twisted. She tiptoed forward and disappeared into the blackness.

TWELVE

FATHER FELIX WAS EXHAUSTED. He was up half the night. His room was like a furnace, he was stuffed from all he had eaten at dinner, doors were slamming all through the night and he was worried.

It wasn't only what he was about to do (under Mrs. Johnston's watchful eye, although he had to admit that he wouldn't mind having her along. There was something about her boldness which was rather comforting. But then that would involve Mrs. Hopwood and wherever she went chaos followed.)

Besides that would mean confiding in Mrs. Johnston and he really couldn't do that. Not if he was going to keep his vow—the confessional seal. And Mrs. Johnston was not the sort of woman who would agree to help unless she had more information. Although, oddly enough, she was there when the man had confessed.

FATHER FELIX HAD come out of the confessional (with the hope of chasing the man down, although that certainly wasn't protocol) when he bumped straight into Amelia Johnston, who for some reason had followed him out of the church. She was a nosy woman and she asked right away what he was doing.

Her questions alerted the man, who had just bared his soul and the man turned around and stared at Mrs. Johnston, with shock and bitterness, before he dashed down the street.

"What was that all about?" In spite of the fact that she was clearly not welcome, she was still curious.

But Father Felix had a question of his own. "What are you doing at church on a Saturday afternoon?"

"I'm setting up the flowers for First Communion. Don't you remember? I'm supposed to be helping Mrs. Hopwood, who didn't even show up. Something about Alex."

"Never mind," Father Felix said quickly.

TOMORROW HE WOULD HAVE some leisure time and then not again for four days. He would have to go to the crypt at least twice, so tomorrow was it. He wasn't looking forward to doing this but he had come so far. Although he was rather hoping he could go no further.

THIRTEEN

Mrs. Hopwood struck a deal with Mrs. Johnston.

After Sapphire disappeared into the night, the teachers marched back into the hotel and demanded to check Sapphire's room. When the sleepy and sulky hotel manager finally agreed to let them in, they found Sapphire in bed. She pretended to have been there the entire night.

Mrs. Hopwood didn't believe her but Mrs. Johnston said it was none of their business.

That surprised Mrs. Hopwood.

Mrs. Johnston was a curious woman, who loved trouble. When Miss Pinkerton was viciously murdered it was Mrs. Johnston who prodded Mrs. Hopwood to help find the killer.

"I'm on vacation," was Mrs. Johnston's explanation, "and while you were taking that long shower..."

"It took a while before the water got hot."

"I read through the rules and regulations concerning the girls. There is nothing that says that they are not allowed to venture outdoors alone."

Mrs. Hopwood and Mrs. Johnston had arrived at the breakfast buffet as they continued to squabble.

"I am quite sure that they are not allowed to leave the premises and wander around Sicily unaccompanied in the middle of the night."

"She didn't leave the premises." Mrs. Johnston put two large pieces of lemon cake on her plate. "She was merely outside of the hotel. She could say she was getting a breath of fresh air. And the time of day is not specified."

Mrs. Hopwood eyed the eggs, which looked runny. "Sapphire looked as though she was waiting for someone."

Mrs. Johnston helped herself to several waffles, put a mound of butter on them and then drowned them in syrup. "We don't know that."

Mrs. Hopwood was tired of arguing and maybe her friend had a point. They were on vacation and they were only responsible for the girls to the extent that they did not get hurt. What happened before they got to Sicily or after the trip was not their concern.

She eyed Father Felix sitting by himself and nursing a cup of coffee. He looked tired and grumpy. She grabbed several eggs, a cup of coffee, a piece of muffin, hobbled over and she sat down beside him. She greeted him in a perky voice. He barely glanced at her.

She stabbed her egg, which was ice-cold and

much too salty. She took a gulp of coffee and almost spit it out. It had a bad aftertaste.

"Instant," Father Felix said.

Mrs. Johnston plopped herself down and began to eat with gusto.

Mrs. Hopwood decided not to waste time on pleasantries. "We have some leisure time today."

"I know what I'm going to do with my leisure time." Mrs. Johnston didn't have any complaints about the waffles, which she was gobbling down. "I'm going to take a nap."

"Sounds good," Father Felix mumbled.

"I want to go to the crypts," Mrs. Hopwood insisted. Mrs. Johnston managed to hiss with a mouth full of syrup while Father Felix seemed to pale.

"Hello." A tall blonde with very white teeth, one green eye and one brown eye, sat down. "My name is Judy."

"Hello, Judy," Mrs. Hopwood, Mrs. Johnston and Father Felix said simultaneously

"I'll be your tour guide."

"You don't look Italian," Mrs. Johnston noted rather irritably.

"I am Sicilian but I was raised in Long Island. I came back her a few years ago. I love Sicily. Even when the weather is dark and gloomy outside, I believe it's always seventy and sunny in Sicily." And she added quickly, "I'm very good at what I do."

Father Felix stared at her and Mrs. Hopwood could almost guess what he was thinking, which would be, *that would be for me to determine.*

Mrs. Hopwood filled the gap by saying, "I have cousins in Long Island. In Floral Park." And then she took a spoonful of her peach yogurt which tasted rather bland.

"No, I'm from further out," Judy said rather quickly.

"Near Jones Beach?"

Mrs. Hopwood didn't miss Father Felix's exasperated sigh and Judy didn't answer. Instead she asked a question of her own. "Is there anything special I should know about the girls?"

Mrs. Hopwood looked at Mrs. Johnston who was looking at her lemon cake.

"Well," Judy paused awkwardly, "I guess then I will see you on the bus, which will be parked in front of the hotel in about twenty minutes. I hope this will be a very happy time for all of us." She rose and sailed away.

"Well, she has a lot of energy," Mrs. Johnston said, spilling crumbs on the tablecloth.

"Why shouldn't she?" Father Felix asked. "She's about sixteen."

Mrs. Hopwood turned towards Father Felix. "Are you going to go to the crypts with me or not?"

"I'll go." His face was expressionless.

"You will?" Mrs. Hopwood was surprised and relieved since she was not about to visit the catacomb by herself.

"Who is going where?" Mrs. Johnston opened her brown tote and threw in a hardboiled egg, some crackers and cheese and an orange.

"We're going to the crypts. Want to come, too?" Mrs. Hopwood asked hopefully.

"Yeah, like I really want to look at a bunch of dead bodies."

Father Felix stood suddenly. "I think we should gather the girls."

"This would be a perfect vacation," Mrs. Johnston moved her chair where it made a loud screeching noise, "if it weren't for those twenty-five girls."

FOURTEEN

AMELIA JOHNSTON MANAGED to sit by herself which was a good thing.

Mrs. Hopwood was seated beside Father Felix, chatting a mile a minute, oblivious to the fact that he seemed totally bored and was glancing out the window.

Judy was incapable of quieting the girls but, unfortunately, that did not stop her from speaking. She began a monologue of the history of Sicily, first owned by the Arabs and then the Normans, followed by Swabians and the Angevins, then the Spanish and finally the Italians. Judy lectured on the sights of Palermo, pointing out the churches, the Palermo Cathedral, the San Giovanni dei Lebbrosi, the Chiesa della Martorana—which no one seemed particularly interested in.

"Unfortunately, Palermo was damaged quite a bit during World War II. You will notice that some of the facades are peeling and some structures are crumbling."

"Then why doesn't someone fix them?" A

bold as brass girl screamed out from the back of the bus.

Judy ignored her. "We'll be riding by the other side of town where you will see a ferverish construction of new buildings."

"Can't wait," someone mumbled.

Amelia Johnston was just about to heave herself to her feet and grab the microphone out of the hands of the incompetent guide when Father Felix leaped up and in his deepest, scariest voice, bellowed, "QUIET!"

Everyone was stunned into silence, even Judy.

"Someone is trying to speak," Father Felix continued to yell, "and you WILL listen. Your parents paid a lot of money for you to visit Sicily and not because they wanted you to have a good time. They wanted you to learn. I can't make you learn. Unfortunately, you are not my students and you do not attend St. Polycarp. But I can make you listen." Mrs. Johnston wondered just how he was going to do that. Father Felix turned towards Judy and then said softly. "You may continue."

And continue she did. Judy went on and on in a bored, tired tone as the bus meandered down the crowded streets of Palermo.

It was obvious to Mrs. Johnston that, although the girls were silent, they were hardly overcome by the charm of the city. Most of them appeared to be dozing or communicating with each other in their own version of sign language.

All except Sapphire.

She was sitting alone. Her face was pressed up against the window and she appeared to be taking in the sights. Although Mrs. Johnston doubted that she was actually seeing anything. Sapphire seemed nervous, jumpy. Something was definitely amiss.

Mrs. Johnston turned her attention to Mrs. Hopwood, who did appear to be listening, although she was probably just daydreaming about all the shoes she was planning to buy. She wasn't even glancing in Sapphire's direction so Mrs. Johnston thought that Mrs. Hopwood had probably forgotten all about Sapphire, in spite of her concern the night before.

Well, maybe Mrs. Johnston should forget about her also. And just when she was about to—Sapphire turned around and stared at Mrs. Johnston. It wasn't just a mere glance, it was more like a glare or maybe just a challenge. It was a look full of anger and bitterness, a furtive, guilty look.

It was a contest and Sapphire lost. After about thirty seconds, she lowered her eyes. But Mrs. Johnston had learned several things. First, Sapphire knew exactly who had seen her in the alley last night. And two, Sapphire Sullivan was definitely up to no good. And finally, Mrs. Johnston had a responsibility to learn exactly what that no good was.

Mrs. Johnston was not one to shirk her duty. But she was a proud woman and she was not about to admit that Mrs. Hopwood had been right all along. She was going to go this alone. Or at least try to.

"You're not going to buy that thing are you?" Mrs. Hopwood scowled in disapproval.

"What's wrong with it? It's a perfectly good wallet. Look how many compartments it has. I can fit my money, my credit cards, my checkbook..."

"And you think you're going to be able to fit that into your fanny pack?"

Mrs. Johnston would not concede. She opened her fanny pack and managed to stuff the wallet in.

"'Cuse me, 'cuse me." A skinny woman with red streaks came up from behind and wagged a bony finger at her.

"Just trying it out. I'll buy it."

The woman smiled, exposing a gold tongue stud.

"It weighs more than you," Mrs. Hopwood argued. "It's heavy."

"That's because it's real leather."

"I'm not convinced of that."

"You don't have to be. You've not buying it." Mrs. Johnston took out her money. A flutter passed her stomach as she realized how quickly her cash was disappearing. But then she picked up a medal of Saint Rosalia. Hadn't Judy said something about Rosalia saving Sicily from the black plague? If Rosalia had saved Sicily, then maybe she could cast some good luck on her.

"I'm telling you buying that fanny pack was a mistake," Mrs. Hopwood said firmly.

"You're talking about mistakes." Mrs. Johnston looked at the sequined gold heels which Mrs. Hopwood had in her hand. "They look like something a Mafia wife would wear."

"I'll take them," Mrs. Hopwood decided.

FIFTEEN

Father Felix rapped on the door.

No one answered. Maybe Mrs. Hopwood changed her mind and was sitting somewhere with Mrs. Johnston having a gelato or a cappuccino with a cassata.

He should be relieved.

He heard movement inside.

Suddenly the door opened and Mrs. Hopwood stood in front of him. She was wearing a red and white polka dot dress with matching red spiked heels. A large white watch dangled from her wrist and huge hoops swung on her ears.

"You can't wear those." He looked down at her shoes.

She stared at him as though he was speaking in a Sicilian dialect.

"You won't be able to walk in those," he repeated.

"We're walking?"

"It's only a mile away." He fumbled in his pocket and pulled out a hotel map.

Mrs. Hopwood was silent.

"Do you still want to go?" he asked.

"Can't we take a taxi?" she asked hopefully.

"Not unless you want to pay for it."

Mrs. Hopwood looked down at her shoes.

"Don't you have a pair of sensible shoes?"

She gazed at him blankly.

"Something you can walk in?"

"For God's sake!" Mrs. Johnston came to the door, wearing some sort of African caftan. "Go or don't go. But stop gabbing. I am trying to get some sleep!"

"Do you have a pair of shoes you can lend her?"

"She's a size bigger than me," Mrs. Hopwood whined.

"You'll still be better off."

Mrs. Johnston was obviously not pleased and Mrs. Hopwood was not grateful, especially when she caught sight of the sensible brown sandals, which even Father Felix had to admit were rather ugly.

"They're going to clash with my red and white outfit," Mrs. Hopwood whined.

"You'll live," he promised.

And off they went.

MUCH TO FATHER FELIX'S dismay, the day had turned chilly and overcast. The skies were gray, threatening a dreary shower of rain. He didn't relish visiting the crypts during a storm, especially while dragging Mrs. Hopwood with him.

Because it soon became clear that Mrs. Hopwood wasn't used to walking in her shoes or anyone else's. She was huffing and puffing, while she attempted to keep up with him and he was hardly moving at all. And she was doing a great deal of grumbling.

"How much farther is this? I think we're lost, that's what I think. Maybe we should save this trip for another day, a sunny day… Does it cost money to get in because I haven't had a chance to change my dollars into euros yet. I don't know if they allow pictures but I brought my camera anyway… I can't imagine how Mrs. Johnston can walk in these sandals. They're giving me blisters. I was better off in my own high heels."

Father Felix muttered now and then, which seemed to satisfy her but didn't shut her up.

Suddenly she stopped. "Look at that, will you?"

They were turning a bend and cars were whizzing by. Even more alarming were the speed of the motorcycles. Traffic signals in Sicily were much like the lights everywhere in Europe—mere suggestions. Vehicles were not inclined to stop and let you cross. And if you ventured too close to the road, there was a very good chance you'd be run down like a dog.

Mrs. Hopwood was awfully close to the road.

Before he could warn her to get out of the way, she stooped down on the side of the curb and lunged toward a brown leather handbag.

It didn't look like anything she'd ever carry.

"Someone lost their pocketbook."

"No one lost their pocketbook." Father Felix shoved Mrs. Hopwood farther into the stone wall and away from the road. "It was probably stolen." She looked at him, puzzled. He didn't really want to explain to her. Mrs. Hopwood tended to exaggerate and be dramatic all on her own. "In Sicily," he paused, "well, really all over Italy and in Europe also, motorcycles come speeding by. If you happen to be standing close to the road and your handbag is on your shoulder, they might very well yank it from you and drive on. When they have stolen your money and sometimes your identity, they dump the bag." He eyed Mrs. Hopwood as she pulled her bright yellow tote bag closer to her hip. He doubted very much if anyone would be able to lift it.

Then she opened the brown bag as though it were on fire. "Well, it smells good, all lemony," she said.

"I'd put it down," Father Felix advised.

Mrs. Hopwood ignored him. Instead she peeked

into it. He looked over her shoulder and spotted some lifesavers, some crumpled tissues, an empty pill bottle, assorted papers and a key chain.

"I guess they got her wallet," Mrs. Hopwood said dryly.

"Let's go." He felt a drop of rain hit his head.

Mrs. Hopwood continued to totter but did not relinquish the bag.

With a quick intake of breath he asked, "Where do you think you're going with that?"

"I think the woman might want her handbag back."

"We don't even know her name," he argued.

"We do. Her name is Phoebe Medina. It was on the prescription pill bottle. And it even had an address right here in Sicily. She's from the town of Camastra."

The rain was coming down heavier now. And here he was standing in a deserted street with Mrs. Hopwood who looked like a blackjack dealer and was behaving like a clown.

"What do you suggest we do?" he asked in a weary tone of voice.

"We could bring it to the Italian police. Maybe they could lift fingerprints from it," she said shrilly.

"So you're going to drag it to the crypt with us?"

"Why not?"

He could think of no answer. "Let's just get going. There are eight thousand bodies waiting for us." And something far more important, he thought.

SIXTEEN

SAPPHIRE COULDN'T IMAGINE why he hadn't shown up. She had left too soon, that was it. And now, how was she supposed to find him? And what if she didn't? She couldn't bear the thought of trying to push the stuff through the airport again. Too harrowing for words.

But she certainly couldn't leave it behind.

She'd have to wait, that's all, and pray that he would call her.

Was it wrong to pray for something like this?

Was it wrong to pray that no one suspected her?

Except that teacher, that Afro-American who kept staring at her with those big black eyes, as though she could see right through her. She had been one of the people in the alley last night but that would mean that the teacher knew she was going to be there and how could that have possibly happened?

Maybe they were on to her. Maybe he got caught and sold her out. Maybe this was all some sort of elaborate set-up.

Was she going to end up in a Sicilian jail? Visions of *Midnight Express* came to mind. A damp, dark cell, eating grasshoppers for dinner, sleeping with rats, socializing with gangsters' wives, who didn't even speak her language.

Sapphire was in way over her head with no way out.

SEVENTEEN

"How much is this going to cost?" Mrs. Hopwood asked the moment she spotted the wicker basket.

The rotund monk sitting behind the basket did not answer or maybe he didn't speak English. Father Felix intervened by silently pointing to the sign which said two euros. Only she didn't have two euros, which was all Mrs. Johnston's fault for telling her to wait until they got to Sicily to exchange their money.

She dug out two dollars and held them up. "Can I use these?" she asked to no one in particular.

Father Felix sighed deeply and threw some coins into the basket.

She promised that she'd exchange the currency as soon as she returned to the hotel even if the rate was high.

"Those hoods are freaking me out," she whispered.

Father Felix looked around. "I don't see any gangsters here."

"I am talking about the hoods on the monk's uniform."

"Habit," Father Felix corrected her, "and they're called Cappuccinos."

"You mean someone named them after a coffee drink?"

"No," Father Felix said in a patronizing tone. "I mean, someone named a coffee drink after them."

"How do you know all this anyway?" Mrs. Hopwood was feeling hungry, hot and hostile.

"I read about it when I was researching the crypt."

Mrs. Hopwood stopped dead in her tracks. "I didn't know that you researched the crypt. When I mentioned it in the taxi, you made it sound as if you never heard of it."

"Just keep walking."

Hobbling, she followed Father Felix down a long, dark, cool underground tunnel, thinking how creepy it was and wondering what happened to all the other tourists. The ceiling was so high, she felt as though she had fallen at the bottom of a well. Maybe this wasn't a good idea. After all, it was so late in the day and this trip would probably be better on a nice sunny morning with a bunch of people who were chatting merrily, emitting collective gasps of awe—and anyway how were they going to get home in the pouring rain?

They landed in a large wide corridor and on either side bodies in various stages of decay were suspended by hooks on the walls. Below lay more bodies in open coffins, dressed in garments that were so ancient they looked like blue tissue paper.

"They are over a hundred years old," Mrs. Hopwood was reading from the brochure. "Look," she gazed up, "an entire family." She pointed to a man and a woman dressed in their Sunday best and then two baby skeletons, little girls in white dresses. "I wonder what happened. A whole family wiped out like that."

A ghostly voice came over the intercom, warning the tourists not to take pictures and then a warning to keep their voices low.

"I think they're talking about you," Father Felix said. "You're too loud. You should have respect for the dead."

Mrs. Hopwood didn't say a word after that. It wasn't the dead that worried her. She didn't want to irritate Father Felix, who would be accompanying her home. So instead she concentrated on the brochure, trying to distinguish the skeletons—and the various sections, which were organized by status and gender. The women were separated from the men, and the virgins, who could be identified because a metal band was wrapped around their skull, were kept apart from the others. There was a section for priests (wearing tattered cassocks and white habits and the cardinals had hats on their heads), and one for professional men, merchants and painters. Soldiers, dressed in moth-eaten parade uniforms, slept in another section.

Their skin was yellow and waxy—their closed eyes sunken and shadowed, their limbs spindly.

Some of them appeared to have died violently—one of them had a bashed-in head. One looked as though there was a knife wound in his suit and then one man was lying on top of another, only instead of a hand, he had a hook.

She turned the corner and landed in an area which was lined with the coffins of children. Maybe they had all died of the black plague, although she remembered something about St. Rosalia saving the Sicilians from the sickness.

All these little children—she thought it was pathetic. She turned to say that to Father Felix, only he wasn't there.

No one was beside her. She was alone in the tunnel, flanked by dead bodies and for a moment she could have sworn that one of the children actually moved.

She was attempted to call out but then she was afraid that someone would tell her to shut up, although that wouldn't be a bad thing because then she would know that someone else was in the building.

But, of course, someone else was in the building. What about that monk? And Father Felix was probably just around the corner.

Except that he wasn't. When she turned the corner and entered another room, all she saw were more dead bodies. She walked straight ahead, determined not to look left or right. Yet she had the distinct feeling that their eyes were following her.

At the end of the hall was a door and, glancing at the brochure, Mrs. Hopwood realized that this was the strainer room, which was where bodies had been embalmed. Because of the underground conditions of the crypt itself and the vinegar inserted into the bodies of the dead, decaying was delayed. In some cases for centuries.

Mrs. Hopwood wasn't sure whether or not she was allowed in the room—and she had no desire to go there.

Stillness had settled over the scene as she felt a flutter of panic.

This is ridiculous, she told herself. I can't possibly be the only one here. And even if I were, all I need to do is find the exit and I'm home free.

Except home was a thousand miles away. How would she possibly get back to the hotel? Even if she could find a taxi, how could she pay him with only American dollars? *Oh my God,* she thought, *this is a nightmare.*

Maybe Father Felix had done this on purpose. He had been acting very peculiarly since they arrived in Sicily. Even Mrs. Johnston had noticed it.

She looked down at her handbag and noticed her cell phone. Suddenly the idea to call him on his own cell occurred to her. Maybe a ringing phone was disrespectful but so was screaming at the top of her lungs, which she was about to do at any moment.

No service.

Silly of her to think there would be. After all, she hadn't signed up for international service. The truth was she hadn't wanted anyone to call her—at least from the States. Seven days without Alex's whining and her husband's demanding had seemed blissful.

Now that didn't sound half-bad.

On the wall she spotted a fire alarm. Well, if worse came to worse, she was going to pull it.

She remembered then about the other handbag belonging to Phoebe. What had happened to it? She had put it down by the entrance while she searched for euros and never picked it up again. Right now that was the least of her problems.

She had three choices. She could stay still and hope someone would find her—or she could walk in circles, hoping she would find someone. Or she could pull the fire alarm.

Someone dimmed the lights.

And she was alone.

EIGHTEEN

MRS. JOHNSTON wasn't quite sure what to do about dinner. They were supposed to be eating at the hotel with the girls but it was going on six and there was no sign of either Mrs. Hopwood or Father Felix. She didn't relish eating with Judy by herself. And also she was a bit worried.

It looked as if it was going to storm. Mrs. Hopwood hated the rain. She was always afraid that her shoes would get wet. Only in this case, it wouldn't be Mrs. Hopwood's shoes but Mrs. Johnston's.

The shoes didn't matter and, after all, her friend was perfectly safe, accompanied by Father Felix, who was the height of sensibility (except for that brief period of time when Mrs. Johnston was convinced he was a serial killer). So in one minute flat, Mrs. Johnston went from being worried to being annoyed. Didn't they realize that she had to eat? Knowing them, they probably decided to ditch the hotel food and were now cozy in some little Italian bistro, enjoying veal and pasta and red wine, while she was alone in the hotel room.

She had tried Mrs. Hopwood several times on her cell but the call wasn't going through. Perhaps she was too far away or she had forgotten to charge her phone or worse still, Mrs. Hopwood hadn't even bothered to sign up for the international plan—and just when Mrs. Johnston thought all was lost—her own cell phone rang and she made a beeline for it.

It was Peter and he sounded far away. He didn't ask how she was or whether or not the flight had been uneventful (Mrs. Johnston guessed he just assumed it was) and being Peter he got right to the point. "I don't want you to panic."

A statement like that brought immediate panic to Mrs. Johnston. "What happened? Are the twins all right?"

"Jeffrey swallowed a penny. You know those coins you are always saving and I tell you just to throw them out."

"They add up. I know someone who bought a car that way. All right, it was a used car but anyway the pennies are always on top of my dresser. In my bank."

"Well, Justin broke the bank. And Jeffrey ate one of the pennies."

"Is he all right?"

"I had to bring him to the emergency room. They said that he'll probably expel the penny when he goes to the bathroom." Peter's tone went from exhaustion to irritation. "I have to look for it."

"Oh." Mrs. Johnston hesitated a moment. "How is the piggy bank?"

"I told you! It's smashed to smithereens. If you had kept it further back on the shelf…"

Mrs. Johnston didn't say what she was thinking, which was simply that it wouldn't have mattered. The boys would have found it. The bank had belonged to her great-grandmother Ruth and had been in the family for generations. And then along came the twins.

There was an uncomfortable silence. Mrs. Johnston could think of nothing more to say. She knew that her husband had resented this trip. But it wasn't as if he had to watch the boys the entire time. Her mother was taking them in the daytime. All he had to do was bathe them and put them to bed (which even Mrs. Johnston had to admit was no easy matter).

Well, she deserved some time off. She worked very hard at St. Polycarp and she was due for a good time. Except she wasn't having one.

"Keep me posted," she finally said.

Peter's only response was a grunt.

"I love you," she added before hanging up. She walked to the window and looked out. There wasn't much to see, just the deserted alley and Sapphire certainly wasn't there now.

She'd have to go down to dinner by herself. Darn that Mrs. Hopwood and Father Felix! She would give them a piece of her mind when she saw them again. Maybe she'd get lucky and they would show up for dinner.

But they never came.

NINETEEN

FATHER FELIX WAS feeling guilty.

He had purposely ditched Mrs. Hopwood because he couldn't have her around while he investigated. If it had been Mrs. Johnston, no force on earth would have separated them but Mrs. Hopwood was easily distracted and now she was somewhere in some room, probably worried and anxious.

If she realized that he left.

He had to find out two things—where the cameras were located (if there were any) and where he could hide when he came back.

He found the cameras easily. They were hanging in the corners of two of the halls. He knew something about cameras because he had them installed two years ago at St. Polycarp—after Mrs. Pinkerton met an untimely end (although he doubted that cameras could have saved her life since she was murdered in the teachers' room). These cameras were old and inexpensive—they could only follow you if you were situated in the middle of the floor. If he managed to flatten himself against the screens—he should be all right. (Although the thought did give him the willies).

He scurried to the section where the priests were buried. All he had written was a number, a number which corresponded to a body. Number 772. He walked quickly and then stopped at the coffin of a skeleton, a skeleton which was half decaying. The dead man had a massive head wound and was missing a hand; at the end of his arm was a suspended hook. He was dressed in a faded blue habit. And under his body Father Felix believed lay a coin worth a quarter of a million dollars.

The problem was how would he find out?

He couldn't just put his hand under the body. There was that mesh screen which separated the skeletons from the spectators.

He knew what he should do. He should tell someone.

But who? The monk at the front desk? And what should he say? That someone confessed a crime to him and then told Father Felix where the loot was hidden. And Father Felix intended to find out if it was true.

And return the loot to its rightful owner?

And what if the monks were dishonest and intended to keep the loot for themselves?

Or what if it wasn't there and Father Felix made a fool of himself?

Or worse than that—he would be breaking the seal of confessional and risking excommunication.

He'd worry about that later.

In the corner at the end of the hall, he saw a door—a closet of some sort. He walked over and tried the knob. It opened easily and he spotted a mop, a broom and a dustpan. A janitor's closet.

"What are you doing?" Someone had approached noiselessly from behind.

Father Felix whipped around and faced a tall, thin monk who did not look unlike one of the skeletons. He had bushy gray hair and a long, sharp nose.

"I'm lost," Father Felix mumbled in Italian, which was the truth. He took a good look at the man, and noticed that, although he was dressed as a monk, his habit was not the same color as the others. "Are you a monk of a different order?"

Father Felix's question seemed to irritate the man. "I'm a monk of the third order. We can be married—we don't live in a monastery and the rules are quite different." Father Felix had heard of such a thing and sometimes he wished that there were priests of the third order. "And I'm the security here. Just to make sure that no one takes pictures or attempts to touch one of the bodies."

"Why would anyone want to do that?" Father Felix felt his heart quicken.

"Some crazy people do things on a dare."

"How long have you been working here?"

"A couple of years—the other guard died. And no, his body is not here. They stopped embalming here in 1871. Although there is still a strainer room. They would put the bodies on terra cotton tubes, remove the insides. Then they would dispose of the body's natural fluids and pump the cadaver full of vinegar."

"Can I see the strainer room?"

The guard shook his head.

"So that's all there is to it, then? Just use vinegar and bodies will remain fresh and free of decay?"

"Certainly not." The man's tone was snippy. "Didn't you read the brochure? It's the crypt itself. The air down here. See that guy over there on the left in the great coat. That's Antonio. They plunged his dead body in an arsenic bath. The poison fossilized him. Giuseppe is underneath him. They immersed his body in quick lime."

"I see." And Father Felix did see. He went over to the screen and peered in, noticing that there was a ticket pinned to the clothing of each body. He also saw pieces of wire.

"What's the wire for," he asked.

The guard shrugged. "Sometimes the bodies, full of poison, vinegar and limestone would fall apart. The arms or the legs, sometimes even the head, would roll off. So they kept the parts together by using wire."

"Nice," Father Felix said dryly.

The guard glanced at his watch and then said in a gloating voice, "You gotta go. We're closing in a few minutes."

Father Felix glanced at the high ceiling. Above him was that small video camera and he was standing smack in the center of the hall. Perhaps he had been drawing too much attention to himself, asking all these questions. So instead he just said, "I have been separated from my friend."

"She's two rooms over."

So they knew where Mrs. Hopwood was.

They knew everything and it occurred to him then that this would not be a simple matter. But then what was? Everything was a battle. He had learned that a long time ago.

"You should get your friend and then leave."

It might have just been Father Felix's imagination but the monk sounded ominous, almost threatening. He didn't wait for an answer but walked away and, as Father Felix took one last look at body #772, he followed the man silently.

He found Mrs. Hopwood, huddled in the corner, her face stricken with fear. "Where were you?" she wailed. "I thought that you left without me.

I had visions of being locked in this horrid place all night."

The monk glared at her and then suddenly said in perfect English, "Such a thing could not occur, Madame."

From the expression on Mrs. Hopwood's face, it was apparent that she was surprised that the monk spoke her language. But in two seconds flat, she suddenly gave him a puzzled look and then said quickly, "Friar, I seem to have misplaced my handbag."

"What are you talking about?" Father Felix quickly intervened. "Your handbag is on your arm."

"Not this handbag. The other one. You know, the one I found on the side of the road."

The monk stared at her with cold, impersonal eyes and then shifted his gaze to Father Felix. He didn't say anything but Father Felix was sure that he was wondering if Mrs. Hopwood was mentally ill.

"Look," she said in a firm voice. "I had two handbags. I put one down when I paid for admission. Or," she turned toward Father Felix, "when he paid for admission. And I forgot to pick it up. It was brown leather, shaped like a moon. Rather a dull handbag—but it was a handbag!"

"We didn't find any such handbag." The monk's voice was clipped and cold.

"Let's go." Father Felix gave Mrs. Hopwood a slight push and then whispered, "It wasn't your handbag in the first place."

The monk stared at them silently. Father Felix was uneasy under the scrutiny as they hurried down the long dark tunnel. I can't believe I have to come back here, Father Felix thought. And how and when?

TWENTY

HE HADN'T CALLED BACK and what was she going to do? Keeping the stuff in her room was dangerous. Her roommate was a girl she had never met before but Sapphire knew that she was one of those goody, nerdy girls, who never wanted to get in trouble.

Therese was named after the little flower and, as far as Sapphire was concerned, that's just what she was. Her background was Sicilian and her parents wanted her to see her homeland.

She was excited to be on the island and talked constantly. If she minded that Sapphire never answered her, it surely didn't show.

"Tomorrow we're going to visit the Palermo Cathedral and I can't wait," Therese said as she offered Sapphire some marzipan which she bought from the store run by Pakistanis across the street. Sapphire shook her head. "I promised my mom I'd take lots of pictures, which is the only reason why she bought me a digital camera. Maybe we can find someone to take a picture of us together."

Sapphire thought it best that there were no pictures of her—period.

"You can use my digital camera, if you want to take pictures, too. When I get them uploaded, I can email them to you. That way we'll both have pictures," Therese said helpfully.

"It's okay." How much longer was she supposed to hang on to the stuff anyway? And what could she do with it? She didn't feel good about hiding it in her room. It was way too chancy.

"But you don't have a camera."

"It's okay," Sapphire repeated.

"Don't your parents want to see pictures? I mean, Sicily is so beautiful and my father…"

"My father is dead. And my mother doesn't give a damn."

Therese was silent. For a moment. "Then why are you here? I mean, you don't go to St. Hilda's."

"Because some stupid lady in our church thought that this was a good idea and took up a collection and then they had a raffle and I won."

"So you don't want to be here," Therese timidly inquired.

"You got it." Sapphire leaned back on the hard twin bed and just before she closed her eyes, she got a glimpse of Therese's hurt expression. For a moment she felt bad.

"I think you are being very ungrateful," Therese

said suddenly and all sympathy vanished from Sapphire's heart. "These people thought they were doing you a favor. And I would think you'd rather be here in Sicily than…"

"Than sweating in my tenement," Sapphire finished the statement for her.

"I didn't say that."

"I'm sweating here, too," Sapphire said. "And I don't care about churches or pretty little villages or wine country or art museums or flea markets or the trash they sell tourists for ten times more than it's worth."

Therese's only response was a deep sigh. "Listen," she said, "we have to be roommates for the next six days. We don't have to be best friends and, after this trip, we don't even have to see each other again. But there is no sense in not being pleasant to one another, is there?"

It was her smile that enraged Sapphire. Here was a girl who could afford to be kind because she came from a loving, stable family. And that's when Sapphire knew exactly what to do with the shit.

TWENTY-ONE

"WHERE HAVE YOU BEEN?" Bursting with anger, Mrs. Johnston confronted Mrs. Hopwood the moment Mrs. Hopwood walked into her hotel room.

"You would not believe what happened."

Apparently Mrs. Johnston was not interested in what happened. "I was left alone, all by myself, to eat with Judy, who is nothing but a chatty Cathy and who didn't shut up for one minute, questioning me about all kinds of personal matters, which were quite frankly none of her business, and then one girl had a headache and was convinced it was a brain tumor and another girl threw up and two girls had an argument which almost resulted in a fist fight!"

"Don't think I had it any better," Mrs. Hopwood argued. "I was actually locked in the crypt by myself."

From the way Mrs. Johnston was eyeing her it was obvious to Mrs. Hopwood that she was doubtful. "It's true! We got there late and we were walking together and he just abandoned me."

"Who?"

"What do you mean, who? Father Felix, that's who. And I think he did it on purpose. I really do. I think he wanted to lose me." Mrs. Hopwood collapsed on the bed, which promptly squeaked. "Someone told me to be quiet."

"So maybe you were embarrassing him."

Mrs. Hopwood glared at her friend, who was in the process of covering her cocoa skin with butter cream. "I am telling you he is up to something," Mrs. Hopwood insisted. "Something is not quite right. I can't put my finger on it…"

Mrs. Johnston sniffed disgruntledly.

"This is from a woman who last year," Mrs. Hopwood reminded her, "thought that Father Felix was a serial killer."

"I never used the word serial killer. I just said murderer. Besides, that's gone and past." Mrs. Johnston threw back the bed covers.

"That's not all," Mrs. Hopwood was on a roll and not about to be stopped. "There was this very creepy monk there, who stole my handbag."

Mrs. Johnston looked at Mrs. Hopwood's yellow tote which was resting on the bureau. "Not that handbag, the one I found on the side of the road. The one that the robbers stole and I found."

Mrs. Johnston pulled the covers over her head. "This is all too complicated for me. I'm going to bed."

Mrs. Hopwood had not undressed. "I'm hungry," she whined.

"Too bad for you," Mrs. Johnston bickered, "you should never have gone to that horrible catacomb. You're just going to have to wait until breakfast. Unless you want to venture out of the hotel by yourself."

Mrs. Hopwood remembered the deserted streets, the motorcycles speeding by ridden by men with dark clothing, the black shadows cast by huge stone statutes. "I guess I'll wait," she mumbled.

She did not say what she was thinking, which was—her stomach growling would probably keep Mrs. Johnston up the entire night.

MRS. HOPWOOD ATE heartily at breakfast and ignored Mrs. Johnston who was ignoring her. Mrs. Hopwood was also ignoring Father Felix because she was still miffed about being left alone in the crypts. And he seemed to be ignoring her because he had to pay for the taxi back to the hotel and, as of yet, she still hadn't changed her American dollars to euros.

She sat beside Mrs. Johnston on the bus but neither spoke. An uncomfortable silence had settled between them. Mrs. Johnston had her eyes closed while Judy rambled on about the background of the cathedral.

When the bus finally stopped, Mrs. Hopwood jerked Mrs. Johnston's T-shirt (which featured a picture of her twin boys).

"It's time to get up," she said.

Mrs. Johnston grunted. "I am so tired," she said. "You kept me up all night. Your stomach was making strange noises."

"I told you that you should have gone with me to get something to eat," Mrs. Hopwood shrugged.

MRS. HOPWOOD MANAGED to climb up the stone steps in her golden wedges and she walked into the massive cathedral and looked around. She had never been in such a huge place. She strained her neck to look up at the forty five foot high ceiling. The paintings depicted the Old Testament and were exquisite. Even she, who knew very little about art, could recognize genius.

Mrs. Johnston had wandered away and Father Felix was kneeling down, lighting a candle. The girls had broken up in small groups and were whispering as they walked.

Sapphire was alone.

Mrs. Hopwood began to walk, noticing the statutes and the coffins (she had enough of those for a while) and the very old pews, the wood scarred and torn. She took note of each statue as she passed and looked down to see the saint it represented. Most of them she had never heard of.

She stopped at a wooden box where a statue of a monk faced her. His thin, narrow face looked strangely familiar and his slightly brutish face seemed at odds with his sweeping monk robe. Under heavy dark brows, his black eyes seemed fierce. His gaze was cast downward and she thought he was rather creepy but, nevertheless, mesmerizing.

She also thought he would make a good picture. She wasn't much of a picture-taker but she had promised her husband that she'd bring back some snapshots. Not that he was interested. He just couldn't understand why she was in Sicily, although she was beginning to wonder the same thing herself.

It took her several seconds to fish the camera from her handbag and as she did so, she couldn't help but think of the other handbag, the one she lost, the one she was convinced that the monk stole. *Well, someone at the crypts must have stolen the bag. But why?*

She finally found her camera and aimed it at the statue of the monk. His eyes met hers and he blinked. She let out a squeak of horror. The movement and whispering in the large cathedral stopped suddenly as everyone stared.

Judy sprinted towards her, looking for the source of commotion. "What's the matter," she asked alarmed.

Mrs. Hopwood pointed at the monk, who was motionless, his eyes cast downward again. "That statue blinked!"

"Well, he's allowed to blink. He's alive."

"I don't understand," Mrs. Hopwood said. "Why is he standing there like that? In that box?"

"He's there to hear confession. Would you like to go to confession?"

"She needs to go to confession," Father Felix was suddenly beside her.

Mrs. Hopwood shook her head.

"I guess I just got spooked," Mrs. Hopwood said, "yesterday when we went to the crypts."

"You went to the crypts?" Judy seemed surprised.

"That wasn't on our tour," Father Felix seemed almost apologetic.

"Well." Judy was appalled. "That's hardly the place for young girls."

"I'm not a young girl," Mrs. Hopwood retaliated.

"I'll say." Father Felix was suddenly beside her. He pushed her slightly towards the rear of the cathedral. "Why must you make a spectacle of yourself wherever you go?"

"I didn't expect that monk to be alive and besides doesn't he look like…"

"Could you please try to keep a low profile?"

Mrs. Hopwood nodded as she looked around. All of the girls were staring at her as well as several tourists. Everyone was watching her, everyone except the monk.

"What is all the shrieking about," Mrs. Johnston asked.

"I thought that man," Mrs. Hopwood pointed to the monk, "was a statue and it turned out that he's alive. She turned to Father Felix. "Don't you think he looks familiar?"

"What I think," he said dryly, "is that you think all monks look alike."

"No, there is something about his face."

Mrs. Johnston shrugged and suddenly checked her cell phone.

"You expecting a call?" Mrs. Hopwood asked.

"Jeffery swallowed a penny. The doctor said we have to wait for it to come out—or rather Peter has to wait for it to come out. As you can imagine, he's not thrilled. Peter, I mean. I doubt if Jeffery knows the difference. I'll feel better, though, when it does comes out. What if it gets caught in his intestines or his colon…"

Mrs. Hopwood, who had gone through the rigors of raising a mischievous son some years ago, merely shrugged and said nonchalantly, "It won't."

Mrs. Johnston just huffed. "Look at her." She pointed to Sapphire. "She's standing alone, like she's waiting for someone."

"Maybe." Mrs. Hopwood was not about to argue. "But I'm more concerned about Father Felix." He was kneeling again, lighting another candle. "Something is wrong. He is very grouchy."

"He is always a little crabby."

"That's true. And when he has the responsibility of running the school on his shoulders, I can understand it. He is constantly telling us how difficult it is. But he is not in school now. He is a thousand miles away. And he's worried about something. And that something has to do with the crypt." Mrs. Johnston frowned. "Don't look at me that way. I am telling you I am dead-on. Something is bothering him."

Mrs. Johnston collapsed in a pew and then glanced down at her cell phone again. "I'm very tired," she said. "Is this the last tour of the day?"

Mrs. Hopwood shook her head. "This afternoon we're going to the town of Enna. A little village in the mountains."

"I can't wait," she said, without any enthusiasm whatsoever.

"WE WANT TO GO DOWN the hill now," one of the girls demanded.

"I promised my grandmother I'd buy her some jewelry and that man is at the bottom of the path."

"I have to go to the bathroom."

"I need water."

"They're worse than second graders," Mrs. Hopwood mumbled.

"Wait a minute," Mrs. Johnston put her hand out. "You have to at least walk into the castle."

"Who says?" A girl with very straight golden hair and very straight white teeth challenged her.

"Yeah, this isn't school," a pretty black girl retaliated.

"Your parents paid a lot of money," Mrs. Hopwood began.

"Yeah, and they don't give squat about any old, decaying castles," the blonde said. "My mother just sent me here because she's on her third honeymoon and I have to bring her back some olive oil."

Mrs. Johnston and Mrs. Hopwood stared at each other resigned.

"And if it leaks all over my clothes, she's buying me a new wardrobe."

"I'd leak it on purpose."

"Be at the bottom of the hill in twenty minutes," Mrs. Johnston warned, "because that's when the bus is leaving and it won't wait. So if your mother wants to see you again…"

"She doesn't care," a bold girl with red streaks shrugged.

"I can understand why," Mrs. Johnston retaliated.

Mrs. Hopwood wasn't going to say what she was thinking, that these weren't students from St. Polycarp. They didn't know Mrs. Johnston and they didn't realize that Mrs. Johnston was, for the most part, a kind, loving person. Except what did it matter? No one would be asking them to chaperone again, which was probably fine with Mrs. Johnston and certainly fine with Mrs. Hopwood and maybe even Father Felix, who had mysteriously disappeared again.

They were thundering down the steep and narrow hill flanked with aloes, daisies, geraniums and oleanders (Mrs. Johnston was taking huge strides while Mrs. Hopwood was struggling with her wedges) when Mrs. Johnston checked her cell phone.

"Can't you give it a rest?" Mrs. Hopwood asked. She was feeling hot and uncomfortable in the bright sunlight.

"Peter called me to tell me that the penny still hasn't come out of Jeffrey."

"How does he know?"

"What do you mean, how does he know?" Two girls came speeding by, almost knocking down Mrs. Hopwood in the process. "He's been fishing for it."

"But you are thousands of miles away," Mrs. Hopwood argued. "There is nothing you can do from here. Look." She stopped suddenly and looked at the low white house with the flat roof. A small wooden door opened and a bent-over woman emerged. Both ladies stopped and peered inside the small living room. Mrs. Hopwood could see a fluffy couch, a huge television, a reclining chair, a cat on a table, beside a cup of tea, and in the corner sat a small compact car.

Judy had caught up with them.

"It looks cozy," Mrs. Hopwood said.

"It's a much simpler life," Judy said. "It's not like being poor in America. Here money doesn't count so much."

Mrs. Johnston nodded. "Sometimes," she said softly, "I wish that I could just live like that. You know, just leave everything behind and become a totally different person."

There were heavy footsteps behind them and, as Mrs. Hopwood turned, she saw Father Felix gliding forward. The sight of him seemed to jar Mrs. Johnston back to the present. "I guess I'm being crazy."

"Who is being crazy?" he asked suddenly.

"She was just saying," Mrs. Hopwood started, "that sometimes she wishes she could run away and live in Sicily."

Mrs. Johnston threw her a scornful glance but Father Felix only commented, "Don't we all?"

"That's why I'm here," Judy said. "Although I have to tell you that I wouldn't mind, living the life of the rich and the famous, even for a day."

"What's important that we really enjoy this trip," Mrs. Hopwood made an effort to sound cheerful. "I mean, who knows when we'll be together again like this. In a few weeks, school begins…"

"Six weeks," Father Felix said quickly.

"Well, let's have a good time."

Mrs. Johnston and Father Felix walked ahead, leaving Mrs. Hopwood to make small talk with Judy (which was difficult to do because the straps on her wedges were digging into her and even going down the hill was causing her to huff and puff). "Do you ever think about going back to the States?" she asked Judy.

Judy shrugged. "Sometimes. Sometimes I think when I have a lot of money, I'll return. Although I don't know how I'm going to get a lot of money being a tour guide in Sicily." She gave a hollow laugh.

"Well, we appreciate you being our guide," Mrs. Hopwood said. "And so far it's been wonderful."

Mrs. Hopwood said that as she followed Mrs. Johnston and Father Felix down the hill. But she didn't say what was really on her mind. She had a bad feeling about this trip.

Maybe it was being alone in the crypt. Maybe it was Father Felix's strange behavior or Mrs. Johnston's distraction over her son. Or maybe it was viewing Sapphire alone in the alley.

She was vowing to have a good time but the truth was that she couldn't wait to get home. It's only five more days, she thought, what could happen in five days?

She was about to find out.

TWENTY-TWO

ALTHOUGH SHE WOULD never admit it to her friend, Mrs. Johnson thought that Mrs. Hopwood had a good point. Who knew when she would be able to take another trip like this? She should enjoy the food and the company, ignore the girls and leave everything behind.

She wasn't about to admit to Mrs. Hopwood either that she, too, had noticed Father Felix had seemed anxious and out of sorts. But, really, neither women had traveled with him, nor, when all was said and done, did they know him socially so maybe when he wasn't in school, he had other things on his mind.

Which wasn't her business—nor was it Mrs. Hopwood's.

And when you came down to it, Sapphire was Sapphire and in five days, she'd be someone else's problem. It was better just to forget about it and enjoy the trip.

She was about to do that. But then Mrs. Hopwood stumbled on to one of her mysteries.

THEY HAD FINISHED eating lunch in an out-of-the-way restaurant. Mrs. Johnston was feeling full and satisfied and a little sleepy. No one had called her from home so she was going to assume all was well a continent away.

Then Mrs. Hopwood, who had been drudging down the hill, puffing, pale and sweaty screamed.

She was walking with Father Felix and they both stopped abruptly. Mrs. Hopwood seemed to be gazing down at an Italian paper. Mrs. Johnston scurried over to have a look. The only photograph she saw was a picture of a hotel.

"What's the matter?" she asked Mrs. Hopwood rather irritably. It seemed to her that Mrs. Hopwood had been screaming all day and she was a little tired of it.

Mrs. Hopwood lifted the paper. "Look," she said shrilly, pointing to some Italian words.

"You don't know how to read Italian," Mrs. Johnston reminded her.

"But her name, it's here." Mrs. Hopwood pushed the paper into Father Felix's face.

"Scusi," an older man who spoke broken English stepped forward, "You buy that?"

"How much?"

"One-half euro."

Mrs. Hopwood looked at Father Felix, who

shook his head and then she turned towards Mrs. Johnston.

"What do you want the paper for," Mrs. Johnston asked. "You can't read it."

Mrs. Hopwood was supposed to go to the bank and exchange some money but she hadn't done it yet and Mrs. Johnston was tired of lending her cash.

"That's her name." She put down the paper reluctantly.

"Whose name?" Mrs. Johnston fished in her pocket. If she had the change, she would lend it but she was not planning to break any bills.

"The woman whose handbag I found, the handbag the monk stole at the crypt."

Father Felix sighed and then mumbled to Mrs. Johnston, "You don't want to know."

"Here." She practically threw the money at Mrs. Hopwood who practically threw the money at the poor Sicilian man who was muttering in Italian under his breath and it didn't sound complimentary.

"What does it say?" Mrs. Hopwood handed the newspaper to Father Felix as they walked down the darkened street and headed for their hotel.

Mrs. Johnston thought that he hesitated and she was betting that he wanted to lie, or at least, tell only a partial truth but he was a priest after all. "It says," he paused, "from what I gather…"

"What does that mean, from what you gather? You know that you can read Italian."

"It seems that this woman—Phoebe Medina is missing."

Mrs. Hopwood screamed loudly.

"You didn't even know her," Mrs. Johnston said.

"I think we should go to the police immediately."

"And tell them what?" Father Felix stopped in front of the hotel.

"We should say that we found her handbag. It could be a clue."

"But we don't have her handbag anymore," he argued.

"We could tell them how we lost it. How one of the monks stole it."

"We don't know that."

The sweat was pouring off of Mrs. Johnston, running a path down between her ample breasts. She was uncomfortably full and the sausage and peppers were coming up on her. She was also exhausted.

"Go to the police," she suggested. "I think it's a good idea." It would mean that Mrs. Hopwood would be out of the room, so she could rest uninterrupted.

"Then you'll come?" she asked hopefully.

"Not me. I don't feel so good."

Mrs. Hopwood looked as though she didn't believe her but she soon turned her attention to Father Felix. "You have to come. You have to translate."

"And what will I tell them?" he asked angrily.

"That I found the handbag of the missing woman."

"And then you lost the handbag of the missing woman."

"I didn't lose it. It was stolen."

"I think you should go," Mrs. Johnston intervened. "It can't hurt. You can tell them where you found it. Maybe that's significant."

Father Felix drew a deep breath and Mrs. Johnston knew that she had won.

"Do you know where the police station even is?" He turned towards Mrs. Hopwood, as though there was a possibility.

"We could find out from the hotel," she suggested.

Father Felix agreed, but begrudgingly.

"Be back in time for supper," was the last thing Mrs. Johnston said before she took to her room.

SHE FELL RIGHT ASLEEP and she slept soundly until she heard a rapping at the door. At first upon awaking in inky darkness, she couldn't remember where she was.

Then it came back to her in a flood—Sicily. And Mrs. Hopwood must have forgotten her keys as usual (she was so irresponsible with keys that Father Felix no longer trusted her with a key to the school).

Mrs. Johnston ambled to her feet, wrapped her caftan around her, rubbed her eyes and went to the door, turning on the flickering light as she did so.

But it was not Mrs. Hopwood who stood on the other side of the door, but two gentlemen with hotel uniforms on and tags identifying them. She blinked twice.

"Are you Amanda Johnston?"

The sight of the two serious-looking men at her door brought terror to Mrs. Johnston's heart. So frightened was she that something might have happened to her twin boys, she didn't even bother correcting the mistaken first name. She nodded, and then with a catch in her throat, managed to whisper, "Is something wrong?"

"Something is definitely wrong," the short, pudgy one snapped. The anger in his voice was a great comfort to her.

Mrs. Hopwood, she thought.

"I don't know how much you and your partner are being paid..."

"She's not my partner." Mrs. Johnston thought it best to severe ties immediately. "Actually, she is not even my friend. We merely teach together."

"And the priest?"

"I barely know him."

"The fact of the matter is one of you is supposed to be in the dining room with the girls at dinner. They are not supposed to eat unaccompanied. Judy is not considered a chaperone. She is employed by the hotel."

"What time is it?" Mrs. Johnston asked innocently.

"Eight o'clock!" The pudgy one leaned towards her in an aggressive manner.

"I'll be right down." She started to close the door.

"It's too late," the tall thin one said in a resigned tone. "They have finished."

"Finished having a food fight." The other man pointed a bony finger at her. "One girl even got a black eye. To say nothing of leaving the dining room like a college cafeteria. We have a great number of customers who have paid a great deal of money to stay at this hotel. It's not fair to them."

"It won't happen again," Mrs. Johnston assured them.

"See that it doesn't. Or we're going to have to file a formal complaint."

Mrs. Johnston didn't know what that meant and she wasn't too concerned about the repercussions, although maybe she should be, because maybe it would end up costing her money.

One thing was for certain.

She was going to kill Mrs. Hopwood.

"IT'S THE SECOND TIME you missed dinner," Mrs. Johnston screamed at her the moment the door opened (there was no need to tell Mrs. Hopwood that she, too, had missed dinner).

"I was trying to find a missing woman." Mrs. Hopwood collapsed on her bed, obviously exhausted. "But I was unsuccessful. It seems as if the missing woman had reported her handbag missing even before she went missing. They think she might be missing because she was involved in some sort of robbery. Something about a missing coin. So I still think there might have been a clue, I mean, the fact that her handbag is missing again."

"I wish I were missing!" Mrs. Johnston snapped. "It simply is not fair. We were supposed to do this together, you and I and Father Felix. And instead, you two are always going off together, as though you have some sort of secret."

Mrs. Hopwood leaped from the bed. "What a

horrid thing to say! I am a married woman and he is a priest, a man of the cloth. You take that back!"

"What I meant to say," Mrs. Johnston stumbled.

"And just for your information, he has been no help whatsoever. He just sat at the police station, looking ashamed as though I were some kind of mentally ill woman. You could have come with us. It's not as if I didn't invite you."

"I had no interest in tracking down someone we don't even know, nor did I want to see the bodies of thousands of dead strangers. Someone has to be accountable for the girls. They're why we're here, you know, why we're having all this fun."

Mrs. Hopwood sank down on the bed again and then said in a sullen voice. "I'm not having very much fun."

"Well, neither am I!" Mrs. Johnston sat down on the chair by the desk, overturning Mrs. Hopwood's neon orange Bermuda shorts. "Look, just don't go off again, that's all."

"I won't."

"I know," it was difficult for Mrs. Johnston to apologize but there was still five days left of the trip, not to speak of the coming year teaching together, "I've been a little on edge. I'm worried about Jeffrey."

"I keep telling you the penny will come out."

Mrs. Johnston ignored the prediction. "Sometimes I just need to be alone."

"So skip breakfast," Mrs. Hopwood said cheerfully.

"That won't work." Mrs. Johnston had already missed dinner. "You haven't eaten, have you?"

Mrs. Hopwood shook her head.

"What do you say we go out for pizza? For dinner tonight they had something called maccheroni con le sarde."

"What's that?" Mrs. Hopwood wrinkled her nose in disgust.

"It's macaroni with sardine sauce. Nice if you like sardines. So anyway, what about going out for pizza?"

"It's not safe here after dark," Mrs. Hopwood argued. "There are motorcycle thieves."

"We'll take Father Felix with us," Mrs. Johnston said.

"You're not wearing that, are you?"

"You mean these sensible tie shoes. Yes, I am. If you want to prance around in high heels, that's your business. But as for me, I'll choose comfort every time."

"That's not what I meant. I meant the fanny pack."

"What do you care? You're not going to walk down the street with me if I have it on? Do you know how many times I've been embarrassed by what you wear—like that hideous coat, you covered with colored square napkins, or that skirt with wrapped-around silk flowers."

"All right, all right." Mrs. Hopwood shoved her out the door.

TWENTY-THREE

FATHER FELIX WAS enjoying the flea market.

For one thing he was by himself. No Mrs. Johnston or Mrs. Hopwood hanging on to him. And the girls had all gone ahead, flashing their euros, determined to buy lots of souvenirs to take home to their families.

Father Felix was not interested in souvenirs. What he was interested in was just walking aimlessly as he viewed the stands with disinterest, stands full of holy pictures and rosaries, of enamel crosses and cheap earrings (most of them made in China), of hats and scarves and mittens and T-shirts, of knock-off designer bags and shoes, of aprons and pot holders and towels, stands full of shrimp and lobsters and scallops, stands full of pears and apples and tomatoes and celery. Every now and then a motorcycle would come speeding down the small, narrow walkway and everyone would screech as they dashed out of the way. And then within seconds, the sidewalks would again be full of meandering tourists.

He had to go back to the crypt. And he had to

go alone. Although how he was going to execute this, he wasn't certain. Tomorrow they had some leisure time coming but someone would have to stay with the girls.

And it wasn't going to be Mrs. Johnston, who had already stayed with the girls twice on her own and was growing very hostile. As though he had been having a good time, stuck in a police station, trying to explain to the bored cops that Mrs. Hopwood tended to be dramatic at best and at worst—psychotic.

He had gone over this again and again in his mind. The way he saw it, he had two choices. He could tell the authorities what he was up to, or he could go it alone. The safer option was, of course, to work with the authorities.

But that would mean breaking the confessional seal, and going against everything he stood for.

Also for some reason he didn't trust the police. Besides, it might all be an elaborate hoax. It was up to him to find out if something was hidden below the body of #772 and, if something was…

He had tried to research the missing coin but there didn't seem to be much in the American papers. Here, though, he might be able to find out more. If he could learn the names of the possible suspects, then maybe he could trace the man who had confessed to him and maybe Father Felix could talk the man into turning himself over to the Sicilian police.

It was worth a try.

He spotted the two teachers. Mrs. Hopwood had stopped to admire a pair of fiery orange shoes, while Mrs. Johnston was browsing in the next booth at tiny T-shirts, probably for her twins.

The moment Mrs. Hopwood saw him she opened a brown paper bag and took out a small silver pick. "Look what I bought," she said proudly.

Father Felix stared. "What is it?" he asked.

"It's a traveling ice pick."

"I don't know what kind of ice it could pick. It's so small."

Mrs. Hopwood shrugged. He imagined that she bought it because it was shiny and bright—and she'd carry it around for show. But Mrs. Hopwood had something else in mind.

"I'm going to put it in my shoe."

He looked down at her apple-green wedges.

"You mean you're going to put it on your shoe— one of your shoes," he asked incredulously.

"Not this shoe. The shoe I showed you in the taxi cab—on the way to the airport."

So much had happened since then he could barely remember the ride.

"The hollow heel screws off?"

"Don't remember. Sorry."

"I think I saw that monk," Mrs. Hopwood said in a frightened tone, "you know the one from the church, maybe the one from the crypt."

"There are a lot of monks in Sicily and, with the robes, they can be difficult to tell apart. Really…"

He was trying to put a stop to what easily could be hysteria, not only for Mrs. Hopwood, but Mrs. Johnston as well when a group of girls, their own girls, came plowing down the sidewalk and bumped right into Mrs. Johnston. She did not react well.

"What is the matter with you?" she lashed out. "This is a public place. You can't go running around and you can't bump into people like that."

The girls surveyed her quietly. This wasn't St. Polycarp, after all, and her authority over them was rather limited.

As though to defy her, Sapphire, who had been standing alone, bumped one of the girls, who bumped another, who bumped a third and they all hit Mrs. Johnston. Had she been a thinner woman, she might have fallen over. But she stood her ground without flinching.

Then they all laughed.

Except Sapphire, who strangely disappeared from view a few minutes later.

Father Felix thought he should do something. The girls obviously had no respect for Mrs. Johnston or Mrs. Hopwood but he was a priest and that might carry some weight.

He hustled over and put on his ferocious principal expression. "Girls! Enough!"

They stopped laughing and stepped back in unison, as though it were some sort of elaborate dance. "If you are to hurt someone, your parents will be liable."

They evidently didn't like this and, as the crowd thinned, the girls muttered under their breath. Mrs. Hopwood was standing motionless with an orange pump in her hand, while Mrs. Johnston threw down the black T-shirts. "I am so worried. They have to find that coin. They just have to."

"Don't worry," Mrs. Hopwood said.

"Because if something should happen and they don't…" The girls were giggling so loudly it was hard to hear. "They're horrid girls and they are behaving badly."

"I agree totally." Suddenly Judy had bounced on the scene and advised Mrs. Johnston not to buy the T-shirts. "The cotton is cheap," she said, "and it won't hold up in American washing machines. And as for those girls, I have to say that they are the wildest group we have ever had. And from a Catholic school, too. They should be ashamed! I don't know who's bringing them up!"

She turned to Mrs. Johnston suddenly. "What were you saying?"

Mrs. Johnston shook her head. She obviously did not want to discuss such a delicate matter with a stranger.

Judy gave an exasperated sign. She watched the girls squealing as they jumped over a crate full of oranges, which were now bouncing down the road.

"At least those girls are not from my parish," Father Felix said with some pride.

"Don't worry. They'll get theirs." Mrs. Johnston threw down the T-shirts.

She said this to Father Felix, as though he didn't know this already, as though it wasn't something he preached every Sunday (even if at times he didn't quite believe it himself).

"They will be punished."

Only it was Mrs. Johnston who ended up being punished.

TWENTY-FOUR

MRS. HOPWOOD HAD NEVER been in such a bizarre place as the Villa Palagonia and she couldn't understand why it was on the tour.

The girls found the 62 monsters fascinating—the hunchbacks playing musical instruments; the dwarfs with grotesque faces, the deformed beggars. They oohed and ahhed over the pictures of 600 bizarre statues. The palace had been owned by a prince, a prince who wished to be surrounded by monsters as he kept his own young, pretty wife a prisoner.

"Look at this," one girl exclaimed, "it's an animal with the head of a lion, the neck of a goose and the body of a lizard!"

"I like this one. It's got the legs of a goat and the tail of a fox!"

"Did you see his bedroom—look at this picture! I want a bedroom just like this! There are toads and spiders and this woman is being eaten by a centipede!"

Mrs. Hopwood was following the girls around, feeling quite sick.

"Here's a picture of St. Francis," Judy whispered to her.

Mrs. Hopwood looked down to find the saint with his hands and feet dangling from his neck.

"I've seen enough," Mrs. Johnson said firmly.

"Me, too," Father Felix trailed behind her, leaving Mrs. Hopwood and Judy with twenty-five girls (well, actually twenty-four because Sapphire was already outside).

"I'm surprised this is on the tour," Mrs. Hopwood said.

"The kids seem to like it—you know, it's gross and kids like gross. At least, I think they do."

Mrs. Hopwood couldn't argue with that.

"You know, I wanted to be a teacher, a kindergarten teacher. It just didn't happen. My marks weren't good enough to get into a decent college."

"I don't think you need to get into a decent college to get a teaching degree. I mean any college…"

"Then I realized that there wasn't enough money in it and I really wanted to make money. You see these television programs about these ordinary girls who marry rich guys and star in reality shows."

"Do you get those shows in Sicily?" Mrs. Hopwood wondered.

"And I read these books about people who come

up with million-dollar inventions and I think why not me?"

"Do you have an invention?"

"My hope is that I'll meet a rich guy and I'll be his tour guide and he'll fall in love with me and we'll live happily ever after in a mansion in Georgia."

Mrs. Hopwood thought that Judy was reading one too many romance books but she was wise enough not to speak, since Judy was ignoring everything she had said so far.

The door burst open and Mrs. Johnston stepped into the crumbling palace. "The bus is here," she said, "and Sapphire has wandered away. Again."

"She's an odd one, that girl," Judy said and Mrs. Hopwood thought that was rather like the pot calling the kettle black. "What's her story?"

"We don't know these girls," Mrs. Johnston said, "and with a little luck we won't see most of them again. Girls," she bellowed, "it's time to leave."

"Where are we going now?"

"Are we going to go to any beaches?"

"When are we going to be able to buy some real jewelry—not that shit on the street?"

"How about some designer clothes?"

Mrs. Hopwood looked at Sapphire, who was making her way onto the bus. She really felt sorry for the girl, who seemed so out of sorts. She obviously wasn't enjoying the trip nor was she bonding with the other girls. Mrs. Hopwood was betting that she didn't go to St. Hilda and she was spending her life on some sort of scholarship. It was painful to watch.

"How many days do we have left?" Mrs. Johnston asked Mrs. Hopwood.

"Too many," Mrs. Hopwood replied.

TWENTY-FIVE

SAPPHIRE HAD FINALLY gotten the call, while she was standing outside at the Villa Palagonia. She picked up her cell quickly, the problem was that she couldn't hear him because there was so much noise in the background and his accent was thick.

And that teacher, the one who was wearing those ridiculous lime-green spike heels was watching, as though she suspected something. As though she was just waiting.

He said something had come up, which was the reason why he hadn't shown up in the alley. Sapphire wondered if it was the long arm of the law and if she was going to be in danger, if this was some sort of set-up. He told her that he'd call her back again with the time and the place.

What was it that her grandmother used to say? In for a penny, in for a pound.

The thought of her grandmother brought tears to her eyes. Her grandmother, so good, so kind, so Catholic. What would she think of what Sapphire was doing now?

She shook the thought from her head almost

immediately. Her grandmother was dead and buried. And if she hadn't eaten all those sweets and been one hundred pounds overweight, she might still be alive. She betrayed Sapphire and left her to fend for herself with her selfish mother and her abusive stepfather.

Sapphire needed money. If for nothing else, to get her sister away from that man.

Well, after tonight she wouldn't have the stuff in her room. She would be home free. She'd have the money and the monkey on her back would have taken off.

She would just have to hope that everything went as planned.

Except Sapphire knew that for her, it seldom did.

TWENTY-SIX

"It's gone."

Mrs. Hopwood looked up from the desk where she was trying to figure out her euro situation and how she could have given the bank two hundred dollars and received a very scant amount of paper in return. Even if she took into account the conversion rate.

"Did you hear me?"

She turned around to face Mrs. Johnston, who was sitting on her bed with the contents of her fanny pack emptied out, including her wallet and the medal of St. Rosalia. "What are you doing?"

"It's gone."

Mrs. Hopwood abandoned her useless task and went over to Mrs. Johnston. She intended to sit on the bed but there was no room. "What's gone?"

"My cell phone."

"Are you sure?" She picked up an Italian newspaper and began to fan herself.

"What do you mean, am I sure?" Mrs. Johnston almost leaped up in anger. "Do you see it here?"

Mrs. Hopwood was going to ignore her crabby

mood, because she knew how Mrs. Johnston hated to lose things (although she had been quite crabby before she lost her cell phone, actually since meeting at the airport).

"When was the last time you had it?"

Mrs. Johnston bit her lip thoughtfully. "The flea market. I remember buying that apron from Grandma Ruth and looking down. I thought at first the phone was ringing and I picked it up but it wasn't."

"Maybe you didn't put it back in that," Mrs. Hopwood couldn't help but grimace, "that fanny pack."

It was the wrong thing to say.

"No, I didn't put it back in my fanny pack. I had it in my hand." Mrs. Johnston hung her head sheepishly. "Because of that wallet I bought yesterday—I couldn't fit it in. Don't you say one word."

"Maybe," Mrs. Hopwood began in a gentle tone, "you dropped it."

Mrs. Johnston stared at her blankly.

"You know—on the ground."

"I didn't drop it," Mrs. Johnston announced dramatically. "It was stolen—right out of my hand."

"Stolen?"

"Don't look so shocked." Mrs. Johnston began to throw items into a tote bag, her wallet, assorted tissues, mints, tour brochures, address books, keys, lipsticks, a blush and a dirty pacifier. "I know exactly when it happened. Remember when you were looking at those hideous orange shoes?"

"I bought them."

"And I was considering those cheap T-shirts. A group of our girls ran into me. I think it was a ploy. I think they wanted to distract me so that they could steal my phone."

"But they all have their own cell phones."

"Why must you always be so argumentative?" Mrs. Johnston hissed indignantly. She zipped up her large bag and threw it on the floor. "Don't you understand my phone wasn't just an average cell phone? It was a BlackBerry."

Mrs. Hopwood didn't respond. Maybe she should go back to figuring out the euro problem. Maybe the bank made a mistake.

"Oh, you are so clueless. A BlackBerry is a very expensive item. Do you know what was in my cell phone? Forget all the personal phone numbers. I had photos in there, of the twins, of Grandma Ruth. I had saved text messages and my agenda and my bank budget. I had downloaded songs." She looked as if she was going to burst out crying.

A wave of sympathy washed through Mrs. Hopwood. She managed to squeeze on the bed and put her arm around Mrs. Johnston's shoulder.

"What if something happens to the twins? Peter will not be able to reach me! Unless" she turned towards Mrs. Hopwood, "he can reach me on your cell phone."

Mrs. Hopwood shook her head. "I'm not getting any service. Remember?"

Mrs. Johnston pushed Mrs. Hopwood's hand away. "A lot of help you are."

"You know it's funny, while I was shopping I thought I saw this monk—he was kind of hidden in the shadows, watching us, watching you. I even mentioned it to Father Felix but he's always trying to convince me that I'm insane."

"So what are you trying to say? That a monk stole my phone?"

"No, it's only that—don't you think," Mrs. Hopwood thought it best to make the suggestion cautiously, "that you should call the carrier of your cell and cancel the service. The person who stole your phone could be racking up your bill."

Mrs. Johnston sprang up. "You're right." She sank down again. "But how am I to do that? I have no phone."

"Across the street," Mrs. Hopwood said. "I heard some tourists talking in the elevator. There's this little shop, run by a couple from Pakistan, and there are phone booths. You can call and it's cheap, only one euro for ten minutes. They also have computers to check your email."

"That's the first good idea you've come up with since—since I've known you. Let's go."

Mrs. Hopwood grabbed her own bag.

"I know who did it, too," Mrs. Johnston said suddenly as she grabbed the room card from the holder by the front door and the room was plunged in darkness. "It was that Sapphire girl. She hates me."

"Why?"

"Who knows why? But this is what we're going to do. First we're going across the street and cancel my account. But," she hesitated, "I'm not even sure of how to do that. I don't have the number of the office."

"I have an idea," Mrs. Hopwood stood in the hall. "First of all, let's go downstairs and get the main number for the hotel. Then you can call Peter. He'll need that number in case of emergency. Not that I think there'll be any emergency," Mrs. Hopwood said quickly. "Then have Peter call and cancel your cell phone."

Mrs. Johnston slammed the door behind her. "All right, that's the second good idea you've come up with. But now I have one." She looked around furtively and then pushed Mrs. Hopwood away from the elevator and towards the stairs. "We've going to get my phone back."

"How?"

"Tonight at dinner I'm going to take my cell phone from Sapphire."

Mrs. Hopwood stared at her friend. "I hardly think Sapphire would be stupid enough to keep your cell phone in her handbag. That is, assuming that she was the one who stole it."

"She stole it." Mrs. Johnston almost pushed Mrs. Hopwood down the stairs. "While they're at supper, we're going to search her room."

Mrs. Hopwood stopped walking. "And how do we do that?"

"Just leave it to me," Mrs. Johnston said.

Mrs. Hopwood didn't like this one bit. For one thing, it meant that she was going to miss her third dinner in a row and she was starving. For another thing, she wasn't at all sure that Sapphire had stolen the phone. Somehow she couldn't believe that Sapphire had done such a thing. Maybe she was just being naive. But more importantly, she thought breaking into someone's room might mean things would spiral out of control.

She couldn't shake the feeling—the persistent sense of impending doom.

TWENTY-SEVEN

FATHER FELIX DIDN'T KNOW what he hoped to find. And it wasn't as though he hadn't looked before. But maybe the internet in Sicily had different information than the internet in United States—especially since the crime had occurred in Sicily.

It was just pure luck that he was able to get access to a computer. Or maybe it wasn't luck at all. Maybe it was God trying to help him. Or maybe someone else.

He found what he was looking for easily and clicked onto the website. There was quite a bit written on the crime. He guessed it had been big news in Sicily—a golden coin worth a quarter of a million dollars stolen from a museum in Palermo.

What he didn't know was that the Sicilian government was offering a twenty-five thousand dollar reward to anyone who could tell them the whereabouts of the coin because the police were baffled.

The police were baffled but Father Felix was not. Not if the man who confessed to him was to be believed. The memory darted through his mind. A man had come huffing and puffing into the confessional and had thrown Father Felix into a loop. Actually he had been snoozing since the people who showed up on Saturdays at noon, and actually ventured inside the little box, were few and far between. Most parishioners, who still confessed, tended to do it on Sunday evenings face to face before bingo. But still it was tradition and tradition was very high in the Catholic Church.

"Bless me, Father, for I have sinned." The man spoke in Italian. Father Felix did not recognize the whisper. "It has been thirty years since my last confession."

Father Felix didn't recognize the profile, either. A stranger from Italy. The man must have known that Father Felix had spent several years working for the Vatican, that he spoke fluent Italian and that's why the man had chosen Father Felix as a confessor. Father Felix sat up straight and tall and leaned his head over to the left. He suspected that this was going to be interesting, not just another list of impure thoughts, and lies to your aging father, or missing Mass, or even an occasional shoplifting, just to prove you could get away with it.

"And this is my sin."

There was a long pause so Father Felix said, "Go ahead, tell me, my son." (Although Father

Felix suspected the man was old enough to be his father.)

"I stole something."

Father Felix was hoping it wasn't going to be a power tool from Home Depot.

"A valuable coin worth two hundred and fifty thousand dollars."

Father Felix was wondering if the man was suffering from some sort of dementia and maybe last night he had seen a movie and he thought he was the thief and in a moment, he would think he was the detective, or maybe the victim.

"I stole it in Sicily and then my father got sick and I had to come here to the United States. I can't believe I did such a thing and that I actually told my wife. Now I am having second thoughts."

Father Felix said nothing.

"Will you forgive me, Father?"

The man started to cough incessantly, which was a good thing, because it gave Father Felix time to think. This certainly called for more than a penance of ten Hail Marys and five Our Fathers.

"Why don't you do the right thing and return the coin?" Father Felix suggested.

"I can't."

"You sold it?"

He saw the man shake his head. "I can't get to it. It's in a crypt."

Father Felix felt a chill run through him.

"In Sicily. There were three other people involved in the theft. But I was the one who actually had the coin. I couldn't keep it on me and I didn't trust my partners. So I hid it in the crypt. The body is number 772. I decided it would be safe there until I got back. I'm afraid of my partners, I'm afraid of the police. I'm afraid of going to hell. Father, I am afraid all the time."

Suddenly the man stopped talking and rose.

Father Felix rose also. "Are you all right?"

"It was a mistake, Father. I am sorry. A lie. All of it, a lie."

Father Felix tried to think of an answer, something to keep the man in the confessional but before he could say anything, the man spoke again.

"The seal of the confessional, you cannot break it, Father. Isn't that so?"

"Well, yes—but…"

"Even if what I told you is true, you can't break it. Am I right?"

"Yes, but…"

Then he was gone. Father Felix sank down in the confessional and, although he shouldn't have done it, he couldn't resist peeking his head out of the door.

He saw a man limping towards the back of the

church. He wanted to call to the man, to catch up to him and then what?

Force him to go to the police.

But then Father Felix ran into Mrs. Johnston, who must have really scared the man away.

"What are you doing?"

Mrs. Hopwood's loud voice jilted him back to the present. She was leaning over his shoulder. His first impulse was to click off the website, which he did as rapidly as he could. But not before he got a glimpse of Mrs. Hopwood's shocked face, as though he had been viewing pornography.

"I had to look something up," he said simply. He spied Mrs. Johnston in a phone booth, her face glistening with sweat. "What is she doing?"

"Calling Peter. She lost her cell phone. Well, actually, she thinks it was stolen." Mrs. Hopwood opened her mouth, as if she was going to add something else and then thought better of it. She sat herself down beside Father Felix, took a deep breath, and then asked, "What's going on?"

He stared at her. "I don't know what you mean."

"I know you. I have taught under you for ten years. You're not yourself. You're edgy, you're mysterious."

He was too tired to deny it.

"I wish you could trust me. I could be such a help to you."

He doubted that, but there was a part of him that so wanted to share the burden.

"I can't tell you," he said simply.

"I would understand. I would. And…" She turned towards Mrs. Johnston and then Mrs. Hopwood began to whisper darkly, "she wouldn't have to know."

"Let me tell you something you will understand. It involves the seal of confession."

She sank back and exhaled loudly. She knew she had lost the battle.

Mrs. Johnston came marching out.

"The penny is still missing."

"You're looking for a penny?" he asked.

"Haven't you been listening? You can be so narcissistic. Jeffrey swallowed a penny. Peter has been monitoring his…"

Father Felix stood suddenly. "Too much information."

"Look, Mrs. Hopwood and I may be late for dinner tonight." She turned towards Mrs. Hopwood who lowered her eyes in obvious embarrassment. "Or we may have to leave early."

He didn't like this. Not at all.

"You have escaped two dinners, left me alone with that ugly mob," she insisted.

He pointed towards Mrs. Hopwood. "She escaped, too. And it wasn't as if I wanted to, trust me, I'd rather eat dinner than be stuck in a police station…what are you going to do?"

Mrs. Hopwood stood. "You're not the only one with secrets," she said. "And believe me, when I tell you, you are better off not knowing."

Father Felix clicked the computer off and walked toward the cashiers. "You're right," he agreed and then thought, being party to one crime was more than enough.

TWENTY-EIGHT

"Did you see that?" Mrs. Johnston snapped down her menu.

Mrs. Hopwood looked up. "There's nothing edible on here. I don't eat veal or pork…"

"Actually the veal is quite tasty," Father Felix reached for a piece of bread.

"How would you know?" Mrs. Johnston couldn't resist the barb. "You missed the last two meals."

"I think it's disgusting the way they treat those animals," Mrs. Hopwood said. "Do you know that a pig has the intelligence of a three-year-old?"

"I'd rather not know." Father Felix reached across for the butter, almost slapping Mrs. Johnston across the face. He turned towards Mrs. Hopwood. "There's a fish choice—tonight's is swordfish."

"I don't like that, either," she sulked.

Mrs. Johnston leaned over and whispered into Mrs. Hopwood's ear. "Did you see Sapphire walk in? She wasn't carrying a purse of any kind, which means that my cell phone must be in her room."

"How do you know she doesn't have it on her?"

"Just look at her."

Mrs. Johnston realized the moment she said it that probably wasn't a good idea. Mrs. Hopwood stood right up and proceeded to stare at Sapphire's halter top and skintight white shorts. Father Felix glanced at her, puzzled and Judy came bouncing along and stared also.

"I see what you mean." Mrs. Hopwood sat down and reached for the bread, momentarily distracted by the scent of honeysuckle. She had always had a nose for scents—she should have worked for a cosmetic company—she imagined being surrounded by beautiful odors all day long. That was so much more appealing than being a teacher.

Was it too late?

"Do you mind if I join you?" Judy sat down.

"We have to go." Mrs. Johnston stood up. "We will be back shortly. Order me the veal and order the fish for Mrs. Hopwood."

"No." Mrs. Hopwood turned towards Father Felix. "Order me a double plate of pasta instead."

"Where are you going?" Judy asked.

"I feel funny asking for a double appetizer," Father Felix said, his mouth thick with bread.

"They won't give you a problem," Mrs. Johnston said simply. "You're a priest."

"Where are you going?" Judy asked.

Mrs. Hopwood looked at Mrs. Johnston. "We have some investigating."

"A mystery?" Judy immediately perked up and the bread that she had just buttered stopped in midair. "I love mysteries!" She actually rubbed her hands together cheerfully.

"Sicily is full of mystery," Mrs. Johnston said. For some reason, which she couldn't really explain, she didn't really like Judy. Her sunny optimism was hard to take and, as childish as it was, Mrs. Johnston wanted to annoy her. "Take the crypt that Father Felix and Mrs. Hopwood visited. Who knows how many bodies are buried there without an autopsy. I mean, if you wanted to hide a body,,,"

"What are you talking about?" Father Felix felt his temper flaring "You didn't even want to go with us."

"Well, I may reconsider."

"Have you ever been there?" Mrs. Hopwood asked Judy.

Judy shrugged. "A couple of times I took some tourist groups. But then we had to stop. Not everyone wants to be reminded of death when they're on vacation. They want to enjoy themselves, make the most of every day."

"That's exactly what we're trying to do." Mrs.

Johnston grabbed Mrs. Hopwood, who was staring at her, mouth agape.

"What's going on?" Mrs. Hopwood repeated as Mrs. Johnston guided her towards the elevator.

"I don't know. I just felt like insulting sunny Sicily. Anyway, we're off to search Sapphire's room."

"But how are we going to get in? You're not thinking of breaking the lock are you because…"

"Of course not. As if I would know how to do something like that. You probably don't realize this, no, how would you? You haven't been at dinner for the last two nights. Anyway, while we're eating dinner, the maids give us fresh towels. I am going to corner one of them and say that we misplaced our key. I'm sure that they'll be happy to let us in. It will be a piece of cake."

"And once you find the cell phone, then what?"

Mrs. Johnston hadn't thought that far ahead. "First things first," she said. "We can do this."

Except it never occurred to Mrs. Johnston that the maid wouldn't speak English.

"MY FRIEND IS a little daffy." Mrs. Johnston couldn't help but notice Mrs. Hopwood's sour expression but it really didn't matter because the maid wasn't understanding anyway. "She locked us out of our room and we need you to open the door for us."

"Pardon?" The maid was standing there with the master key in her hand, with a tray of towels and a huge trash bag. It took all Mrs. Johnston had not to grab the keys away from the silly woman.

"We are locked out of our rooms." Mrs. Johnston was now shouting, as though the maid were deaf and not merely understanding English. "We need you to open our door for us."

The maid shrugged her shoulders and in a pouting manner turned around to walk away, muttering something inaudible and rebellious. But Mrs. Johnston was not to be dissuaded. She marched up to Room 23 and pointed to the door. She jiggled it back and forth and then tapped the maid on the shoulder.

"She's probably waiting for a tip," Mrs. Hopwood suggested.

Mrs. Johnston, who was on a rather tight budget, was not about to give the maid a tip, especially when she had such a bad attitude. However, from around the corner, she heard a voice which paralyzed her with fright. It belonged to the man who had come to her room and complained about her absence at dinner. He would know instantly that she was asking for entrance to a room, which wasn't her own.

Mrs. Johnston dug into her jeans and pulled out two crumpled two-euro bills. It was much too much but she was running out of time. She handed the bills to the maid and then said, "Please."

The maid didn't hesitate. She took out the master key and opened the door. Mrs. Johnston could see the panic in Mrs. Hopwood's wide, frightened eyes because she didn't understand any of it and, as far as Mrs. Johnston was concerned, she wasn't about to.

Mrs. Johnston shoved Mrs. Hopwood into the room and slammed the door.

Half of the room looked as if a cyclone had hit it. The bed by the window was piled with clothing and littered with papers and candy wrappers and cigarette butts. Mrs. Johnston knew exactly which bed belonged to which girl.

"What are we looking for?" Mrs. Hopwood asked innocently as she looked around.

"My cell phone!" Mrs. Johnston snapped. "What do you think we're doing in here? That girl stole my cell phone."

Mrs. Hopwood looked doubtful.

"Don't say she didn't. I know that she did."

Mrs. Hopwood might be hesitant. Mrs. Johnston was not. She started with the open suitcase. There wasn't much in it, probably because most of the contents were on the floor. She picked up a pair of sweat pants, two stained T-shirts and a raggedy pair of slippers. Stuck in the back of the suitcase was a photograph.

Mrs. Johnston picked it up.

Sapphire was a pretty girl. Mrs. Johnston had to admit it, even if she was a thief. She was smiling with nice, white, bright teeth and her blue eyes were crystal clear, her hair a natural golden blonde. She was flanked by two others, one an older version of Sapphire, older and brassier. This woman's eyes were faded, her hair dyed to a platinum blonde. She looked hard and bitter. Mrs. Johnston felt as though she were looking into the future. On the left of Sapphire was a younger girl, with mousy brown hair and sad eyes covered with glasses. No one in the photo was smiling.

"What's that?" Mrs. Hopwood looked over Mrs. Johnston's shoulder.

"Not what we're looking for." For some reason the photograph made Mrs. Johnston uncomfortable. She stuffed it into the pocket of the suitcase. "That's her roommate's suitcase. You don't have to look through that. It won't be in there. Why don't you try the bathroom?"

Mrs. Hopwood was staring in the suitcase as though she had just seen a mouse.

"God, the roommate must sweat a lot."

"Why would you say that?"

"Because she has so much deodorant." Mrs. Hopwood held six push-up sticks.

Mrs. Johnston grabbed them away from her. "Give me these," she said and then she promptly rolled one up. Not to her surprise, the deodorant actually was less than an inch. And hidden below was a stash of marijuana.

"What's going on?" Mrs. Hopwood paled.

"Isn't it obvious? This girl is smuggling drugs."

"Are you sure?"

Mrs. Johnston drew a deep breath. She hated the way Mrs. Hopwood always doubted her. It was insulting. "What do you mean—am I sure? See for yourself?" She shoved the plastic container in Mrs. Hopwood's face.

Mrs. Hopwood quickly recoiled. "I'd rather not," she said dryly. And then she swallowed hard when she heard voices outside the door.

"But I thought I was in the wrong suitcase. I mean, if this is the roommate's suitcase," Mrs. Hopwood said stupidly.

"You *were* in the wrong suitcase," Mrs. Johnston shut the light off, "if you were looking for my cell phone. Come on, we have to get out of here."

"You're taking all of those?"

"I'm not leaving them here. This is illegal. If she gets caught with these…"

"Who is she?"

Mrs. Johnston did not know who she was. She had no idea who was sharing the room with Sapphire, somebody equally dishonest, or maybe not equally at all. Obviously a drug dealer. She would have to look at the list.

She opened the door cautiously and peeked out into the hall. Two girls were coming towards them.

"What if *you* get caught with those?" Mrs. Hopwood asked loudly.

"Be quiet!" She pushed Mrs. Hopwood into the hall. "I won't get caught. But we have to figure out what to do."

"I don't like this," Mrs. Hopwood said again, much too loudly. "I don't like this at all."

"Neither do I," Mrs. Johnston agreed. "Neither do I."

TWENTY-NINE

IT WAS ALL SET.

He had finally called and tomorrow night she was going to get rid of the drugs.

All she had to do was meet him on the corner, make the exchange and he would pay her, in euros, of course, but she could settle all that when she got home. It would be such a relief to have this monkey off her back.

She waited until Therese was in the bathroom and then she opened Therese's suitcase. She looked in the pocket where she had hidden the bottles. They weren't there.

At first she couldn't believe it. She actually dumped the suitcase out on the bed but it was a useless gesture. There were too many bottles to be hidden.

Therese must have found them, and puzzled, might have even thrown them away. How stupid Sapphire was to hide the drugs in someone else's belongings! But it had only been twenty-four hours. Maybe they were still in the trash.

"What are you doing?"

Sapphire whipped around and saw Therese standing there with a towel on her head, clothed in a white, fluffy terry-cloth robe. For a moment Sapphire was furious. It bothered her that, even coming from the shower, Therese reeked of money. She had the indefinable air of being well cared for, even adored. She would never have to do what Sapphire had been forced to do and she would never find herself in Sapphire's situation.

"I asked, what are you doing?"

But Sapphire had a question of her own.

"Where are they?"

"Where are what?"

"My deodorants."

If Therese was acting, then Sapphire had to admit that she was doing a decent job.

"Why would I know where your deodorant is?"

"Because I put them in your suitcase."

"How many deodorants were there and why did you put them in my suitcase?"

Sapphire couldn't think of an answer fast enough so she merely said, "I want them back. I need them back."

Therese shrugged her shoulders, apparently, losing interest. She retreated into the bathroom. Sapphire followed her. "I need my deodorants," she insisted.

"You can use mine." The stupid girl reached into her makeup bag.

"I want MINE."

"Well, there is a drugstore right down the street. You can always buy more—if you want a particular brand…"

"It wasn't just about the deodorant!" Sapphire snapped. "There was something else hidden in there. Something I need."

Therese, looking confused and frightened, took the towel off her head and stared at Sapphire.

"Please."

"But I don't have them, honest. Maybe the maid took them. I'm missing my Creed perfume. I could swear I packed it but maybe I forgot. Do you think you might have forgotten to pack them because sometimes when you could swear that you did something…" Therese asked hopefully.

Sapphire sank down to the toilet seat. Therese didn't have the bottles. She was too dumb to lie.

"What did you hide?" Therese questioned suddenly, her blue eyes wide with fear.

Sapphire shook her head.

"Maybe…" Therese bit her lip thoughtfully.

Sapphire jumped up. "Maybe what?"

"Tonight coming back from dinner, I thought I saw our chaperones, you know that heavyset lady and that other one, the one who wears those horrible bright pink shoes, I think they were coming out of our room. Is that possible?"

Sapphire didn't answer. Of course, it was possible, although how those two women knew what she was up to was beyond her. But they had seen her in the alley and they must have suspected something, or they wouldn't have been spying on her in the first place.

"Is it some kind of illegal drug?" Therese whispered.

"Don't ask any questions," Sapphire said. "And don't say anything about this, either. If you do, you could be in big trouble, as big a trouble as I'm in right now."

"You're right," Therese picked up the blow dryer. "You know, I didn't even want to come to Sicily. All my friends were going to Spain and my parents forced me. They sent me all the way over here just to take pictures and connect with my ancestors. Well, I don't feel any connection at all and my digital camera is broken."

Did she expect Sapphire to feel sorry for her?

Sapphire went into the bedroom and collapsed on her bed, forcing herself to breathe deeply. What was she going to do? The man would be expecting to meet her in just a few hours and she was supposed to deliver the goods. If she didn't have them—well, there would be trouble on both ends, her contact at home and her contact in Sicily.

At the very least, she would be expected to pay for the lost merchandise, which she couldn't do. And the worst-case scenario—she didn't want to think about the worst-case scenario—she had to get those bottles back. But how? Chances are those two busybodies had already gone to the authorities.

One thing was for sure. She couldn't hang around here just waiting for the axe to fall.

Before Therese could ask any more questions, Sapphire crept out of the room.

THIRTY

FATHER FELIX WAS enjoying a glass of grappa when he heard a knock.

With a great deal of reluctance, he rose and opened the door.

"We have to talk to you," Mrs. Johnston said, standing in the hall with a hesitant Mrs. Hopwood.

It wasn't good. It was never good when the two teachers were together and needed to talk to him. Mrs. Johnston didn't even bother to wait for a response. She shoved Mrs. Hopwood into his room and closed the door.

The moment she spotted the liquor, her eyes lit up and she looked at him beseechingly.

"I was trying to unwind." Although he certainly didn't need to explain himself to these two imaginative women.

"I'd like to unwind." Mrs. Johnston made herself at home by plopping on his bed. "Do you think I could have a sip?"

He reached for a cup and poured her a good amount and then gestured to Mrs. Hopwood, which he did only out of politeness, because he knew that she didn't drink. "Do you have any chocolate?" she asked hopefully.

He did. He had bought a box at a local sweet store but he was planning to bring the candy home to his sister, so he wasn't about to open it. Instead of lying, he merely asked, "It's after nine, ladies, and I'm really tired. And why do I feel that you are the messengers of bad news?"

Mrs. Johnston took a gulp of grappa and then, with her other hand, reached into her tote bag, and displayed several bottles of deodorant.

"Are you trying to tell me—and not too subtly either—that I smell?" His brain felt sluggish from food and wine.

"This isn't about deodorant," Mrs. Johnston said firmly.

"Marijuana is hidden on the bottom of these containers," Mrs. Hopwood intervened. "We found them in one of the girls' rooms."

Mrs. Johnston glared at her, although Father Felix wasn't sure if it was because she had spoiled the climax of the story or because he was now going to ask what they were doing in the girls' rooms.

"We were looking for my cell phone," Mrs. Johnston answered the question, before he had a chance to ask it. "I'm convinced that Sapphire took it when she ran into me—on purpose, I might add."

"Did you find the cell phone?"

"We didn't have time to look," Mrs. Johnston said quickly.

"Besides, we didn't even find this among Sapphire's belongings," Mrs. Hopwood said quickly. "It was with the other girl's, her roommate. I think her name is Therese."

Father Felix poured himself another half glass of grappa and slouched in his chair.

"So," Mrs. Johnston helped herself to another glass, as well. "What do you suggest we do?"

"Listen, ladies, we are not at St. Polycarp. I am not the principal. I am not in charge."

"We realize that." Mrs. Johnston leaned forward. "But I thought we could go talk to her—all together. And I certainly think it would be helpful to have a man of the cloth with us. She might be more respectful."

"Or more nervous," Mrs. Hopwood interrupted.

"Can we do this tomorrow? It's late."

"I guarantee you, she'll still be up," Mrs. Johnston said and then added in her stern seventh-grade teacher voice, "I don't think waiting until the morning would be advisable. For one thing, Therese is sure to notice that the marijuana is missing and she might get desperate, especially if she needs a fix."

"Or if she needs to sell it," Mrs. Hopwood said.

Mrs. Johnston stared at her silently and then said, "Do you see our problem?"

Father Felix finished the last of his liquor, feeling hostile. He had enough to worry about with the stolen coin buried in the crypt and now he had to contend with drug dealing. It was a mistake to invite Mrs. Johnston and Mrs. Hopwood on this trip. Where they went trouble followed. It was inevitable.

As though she could read his mind, Mrs. Johnston suddenly hissed, "Don't you dare blame us! You were the one who found this tour and we can't be responsible if you brought along drug-dealing girls."

"You should have never gone poking your noses where they didn't belong," he retorted. "Who told you to break into their room?"

"The damage is done," Mrs. Hopwood said simply. "The most we can do now is to try to talk some sense into Therese."

Mrs. Johnston opened the door and made a sweeping gesture. "After you," she said to Father Felix.

He may have gone out of the door first, but she

clearly led the way. They clambered to room 23 and Mrs. Johnston rapped loudly.

A few seconds later a frazzled girl with a long triangle face and narrow shoulders, dressed in a skimpy nightgown, opened the door a crack.

"Can we come in for a moment?" Mrs. Hopwood asked politely.

"I guess." The girl didn't seem thrilled.

Father Felix was wishing that she would put something on. You could see right through the sheer fabric and he was trying not to look, concentrating on the floor. Out of the corner of his eye, he saw Mrs. Johnston hold up one of the deodorant bottles. He wondered how she was going to explain having the bottle. It turned out that she didn't have to.

"It's not mine," Therese said right away. "It's Sapphire's. For some reason she hid a bunch of them in my suitcase and then she accused me of stealing them. She was really frantic, when they disappeared."

"Where is she now?" Father Felix asked.

"Not here. She left when I was in the bathroom. I think she's in some kind of terrible trouble. But I really don't want to get involved. I didn't even want to come to Sicily. I wanted to go to the Costa del Sol with my friends but my mother is Sicilian and she…"

"Is there anything else you can tell us?" Mrs. Johnston promptly intervened.

Therese shook her head. "Do you think I could change rooms? Maybe someone will come looking for her in the middle of the night and I'll get axed instead of her."

"Don't let your imagination run away from you," Father Felix managed to sound stern, but he had to admit that Therese had a point—except did he really need all this aggravation?

"We should have guessed it was Sapphire," Mrs. Johnston muttered as she headed for the door. Suddenly she whipped around. "One last question," she said. "Did you see any strange cell phones around?"

Therese stared blankly.

"Mrs. Johnston is missing her cell phone," Mrs. Hopwood explained. "Maybe Sapphire picked it up—by accident."

"I don't know anything about a cell phone. How soon can you let me know about the room?"

No one answered her. There was nothing to say as they walked down the corridor. Finally Mrs. Hopwood broke the silence. "We have to speak to Sapphire."

"In the morning." Father Felix needed another glass of grappa.

"I just hope she comes back," Mrs. Johnston said dryly.

THIRTY-ONE

"I DON'T KNOW WHY that television has to be on." Mrs. Johnston had a headache—she was utterly exhausted and ready for bed.

"I can't fall asleep without the drone." Mrs. Hopwood didn't look sleepy at all. She was actually sitting up, wearing emerald-green silk pajamas, propped against the pillows, flipping feverishly through pictures in an Italian fashion magazine.

"But the newscaster is speaking in Italian," Mrs. Johnston argued, "and you can't understand a word that they're saying."

"It's the sound. How do you feel about caged heels?"

"What?" Mrs. Johnston lifted her pillow and pounded on it several times.

"You know—they have spaces like little cages. They're all the rage here—actually I think it started in Paris."

"I'd like to put *you* in a cold and barren cage. God, why didn't someone tell me how hot Sicily is in July? I swear I would have reconsidered. At least could you turn the light off?"

"Then I won't be able to read—I mean, look at the pictures."

"Then turn the television off." Mrs. Johnston was reaching over the night table for the remote control when she spotted a picture flashing on the news.

"That man," Mrs. Johnston stopped and stared, "that's the man I saw confessing to Father Felix."

Mrs. Hopwood put down the magazine. "Don't you think that this is all too coincidental? A man confesses and I'm assuming that he's confessing some sort of crime and then the next thing you know, we're all bound for Sicily. Father Felix must have come here to find him and convince him to turn himself in. Although I don't know how Father Felix expects to find this criminal in Sicily…"

"Will you please be quiet? I can't hear."

"But you can't hear anyway, since you don't speak Italian."

Mrs. Johnston moved closer to the television. "Maybe they'll show some more pictures."

"Oh my God!" Mrs. Hopwood threw down the magazine.

"What's the matter?" Mrs. Johnston asked in a weary voice. No doubt Mrs. Hopwood had read about some out-of-the-way place where the caged shoes were now on sale.

"That name—that newscaster just said."

"You don't understand Italian," Mrs. Johnston reminded her.

"I can understand a name. Medina. That was the man's name."

"So what?"

"Don't you remember how we found that purse—Father Felix and I—on the way to the crypts? It belonged to a Phoebe Medina."

Mrs. Johnston felt her heart quicken. "What happened to the purse?" she asked breathlessly.

"I told you! It was stolen at the crypt. A monk took it and never gave it back. You never listen to me when I try to tell you stories."

"That's because there are so many stories. Although I must admit that this one is interesting."

"And now the woman is missing. I read about it in the paper. Or rather Father Felix read about it. Should we tell him about this?" Mrs. Hopwood wondered.

Mrs. Johnston shook her head. "Not yet. I wonder why Father Felix doesn't just go to the police."

"He can't," Mrs. Hopwood said. "You know the seal of confession and all."

"Well, if we should find out…"

"And how do we do that?" Mrs. Hopwood asked.

Mrs. Johnston didn't reply to a question she had

no answer to. "We are not under any obligation to any seal. So if we should investigate…"

"Sounds dangerous to me." Mrs. Hopwood finally turned off the light.

"And since when are you afraid of danger?" Mrs. Johnston challenged her.

THIRTY-TWO

"So what's with your friend?" Judy, holding a plate of lemon poppy cake and a hard-boiled egg, plopped down beside Mrs. Hopwood.

Mrs. Hopwood couldn't think of an answer right away so she merely said, "She's running a little late today."

"No, that's not what I meant. Something's bothering her. I can tell. She's not herself." Considering that Judy had only known Mrs. Johnston for a few days, Mrs. Hopwood thought that this was a rather audacious remark. "I just thought I could help."

"Another mystery," Mrs. Hopwood muttered, her mouth full of muffin.

Mrs. Hopwood thought that this was a rather innocuous remark but Judy perked right up. "Was that why she was reading the newspaper yesterday?"

Mrs. Hopwood immediately got on the defensive. "Well, she wasn't really reading it. Actually she can't read anything at all in Italian. Father

Felix was translating. Did you ever hear of Phoebe Medina?"

Judy shrugged. "Can't say I have. Are you using that strawberry jam?"

Mrs. Hopwood was planning to, but she handed it over anyway. "Anyway, Mrs. Johnston thinks that she saw this man…"

"Good morning." Mrs. Johnston glanced at Judy as she sat down. "Are you talking about me?"

"I was just telling her about the man you saw running from Father Felix's confessional, who was on the television last night."

Mrs. Johnston shot a death look at Mrs. Hopwood.

Judy sensed the tension and asked, "Would you excuse me? I need to get a cup of Sanka."

"You're not supposed to be talking about our business to complete strangers. What's the matter with you?" Annoyance and surprise were in her voice.

"Just trying to make conversation." Mrs. Hopwood took a bite out of her dry corn muffin.

Mrs. Johnston began to look around.

"She's not here." She had beaten Mrs. Johnston down to breakfast just for the sole purpose of asking Therese if Sapphire had ever come home. She hadn't.

"Can I have my coffee first?" Mrs. Johnston

sank down and scowled as she swallowed what Mrs. Hopwood knew to be bitter, lukewarm and instant.

"What are we going to do?" Mrs. Hopwood was worried.

"We're going to have to go to the Sicilian police."

That was precisely what worried Mrs. Hopwood. She didn't think that the Sicilian police had been particularly warm or kind or sympathetic when she told them about the handbag, and the thought of visiting the local precinct again was not a welcome one. Maybe she could just send Mrs. Johnston and Father Felix, who bore the burden of speaking the language.

"We're probably all going to get sued." Mrs. Johnston stabbed her runny fried egg with a butter knife.

"Sued?" Her corn muffin was suspended in midair.

"I wouldn't be surprised if you lost your condo and your car."

Now Mrs. Hopwood was really worried. "How is this our fault?"

"Because we are responsible for those girls. It's as simple as that. We signed a contract…" She stopped abruptly as she saw Father Felix heading towards them, carrying a cup of tea.

"Is that all you're going to eat?" Mrs. Hopwood thought he was going to need a lot of nourishment to get through the day.

His only answer was a glare.

"She never came back." Mrs. Johnston stuffed a banana in her mouth.

"She thinks we should go to the police," Mrs. Hopwood added. From the look on Father Felix's face, Mrs. Hopwood knew that he, also, did not want to involve the authorities.

"Maybe she met a guy and she spent the night with him," Father Felix suggested.

Mrs. Johnston shook her head. "That might be a possibility but we found drugs, remember? And she was probably set to meet the guy and do an exchange and when she didn't show up with the merchandise…"

Mrs. Hopwood knew where this was heading and she said, "Then you're to blame. You shouldn't have taken the drugs."

"Oh, I should have just let her deal in a foreign country. Is that what you're suggesting? Don't make me try and feel guilty because it won't work!"

"Enough!" Father Felix put his hand on his head as though it ached. He leaned over and began to whisper. "If we go to the police, this is going to turn into a media circus. Girl Disappears On School Trip. And she could still show up…"

"Well, how long are we supposed to wait?" Mrs. Johnston fired at him. "If we don't report it right away, then they'll say we were negligent, that we were trying to keep it quiet for our own reasons. They might even think that we're involved somehow."

"Especially since you have the drugs." Mrs. Hopwood could not resist the barb.

Father Felix released a deep sigh. "Do you mind if I get something to eat?" He rose.

"Look, I'm really worried," Mrs. Hopwood said. "That girl, well, somehow she is pathetic. What if something really happened to her? And we're just standing around, thinking of ourselves. It doesn't seem right. Oh God, here comes Judy again." Mrs. Hopwood could not bear her cheeriness now. She could pretend that everything was fine and they were all having a great time.

"I've got an idea," Mrs. Johnston rose suddenly and gestured to Mrs. Hopwood to rise also before Judy could plunk herself down. "Let me go back and search through Sapphire's things. I'll ask Therese to open the door for me. Maybe I'll find something, a clue as to where she was going. It's worth a try. You stay here with Father Felix and Judy."

The thought struck Mrs. Hopwood suddenly. "What if in the meantime she talks?"

"Who? Judy?"

"No, Therese." Mrs. Hopwood glanced at Therese who was chatting with a pretty black girl and they both looked rather serious.

"She seems as if she's easily scared," Mrs. Johnston said. "I'll scare her some more."

That Mrs. Johnston was more than capable of doing.

Mrs. Hopwood helped herself to some canned fruit and a piece of lemon bread and headed for the table just as Judy sat down, smiling, displaying her very white teeth.

"How are we today? Are we looking forward to our trip to Corleone?"

"Can't wait," Mrs. Hopwood said without any enthusiasm whatsoever.

"Where is your friend?"

"Um," Mrs. Hopwood made an effort to think quickly. "She had to go back for something."

"Listen, I don't mean to be nosy. But I've been a tour guide for a little while and I'm sensing— some kind of—well, how should I say it, discord?"

"That's just us," Mrs. Hopwood answered quickly. "Mrs. Johnston and I and Father Felix, well, we've been through a lot together—murder and robberies and we're a little on edge."

"Murder? Robbery?" Judy exclaimed, looking rather alarmed.

"That was a few years ago," Father Felix said quickly as he sat down.

"Well, it's only," Judy hesitated, "that if something is going on with the girls, something, I should know about, well, it's possible that I could help."

For some reason Father Felix flushed and then Mrs. Hopwood got a terrible coughing spell.

Everyone stared at her as she coughed until Father Felix stuck a glass of apple juice in front of her, but it was more in annoyance than in sympathy.

"I don't know what you mean," Father Felix said, but even Mrs. Hopwood didn't think he sounded very convincing. "We all love Sicily and we're all having a good time."

Mrs. Hopwood took a gulp of the sour juice and then said "Everything is good." She was thinking that she just might need to confess to that monk after all and Father Felix should come with her. "As you say, Judy, it's always seventy and sunny in Sicily."

SHE WAS SITTING ON the bus with Father Felix when Judy did the head count. It didn't take Judy long to realize that someone was missing.

"It's that girl, Sapphire," someone shouted from the back of the bus.

"She's somewhere else," Father Felix said.

"Oh, okay." Judy seemed suspicious.

"I thought you were a priest," Mrs. Hopwood said.

"I am a priest. And I didn't lie, did I? She is somewhere else. I wish I were somewhere else."

Mrs. Hopwood didn't say what was on her mind. She wished that she were somewhere else also.

"She's not coming?" Judy suddenly asked, frowning thoughtfully.

"Who?" Mrs. Hopwood looked up.

"The other chaperone?"

"Here I am." Mrs. Johnston was climbing the stairs of the bus, looking all out of breath, the sweat pouring off her cocoa skin. "Sorry."

Mrs. Hopwood rose, intending to sit with Mrs. Johnston and leave Father Felix in the dust.

"Stay where you are," Mrs. Johnston said as the bus lurched forward and almost put Mrs. Johnston in Mrs. Hopwood's lap. "I need to be alone. Guess what I found?"

Mrs. Hopwood and Father Felix looked at each other. It could be anything—but it obviously wasn't Sapphire.

Mrs. Johnston held up a notebook with pretty daisies on the cardboard cover. "It's her diary."

"I don't think you should read that." She turned towards Father Felix for support. "Do you think she should read that?"

"You're kidding, right?" Mrs. Johnston asked incredulously as she made her way to the back of the bus and scooted into two seats, resting her feet on the empty space.

Mrs. Hopwood watched her reading as Judy lectured on the many sights of Sicily. It seemed to her that Judy was getting mighty suspicious. What if Judy reported them to the authorities and there was a raid and the Sicilian police found the drugs in Mrs. Johnston's room and they all ended up in jail. Mrs. Hopwood better be nice to Judy. She could be trouble and they were in enough trouble already.

WHEN THEY WERE IN the Duomo Cathedral, Mrs. Johnston sat in the back and kept on reading. Mrs. Hopwood thought that the diary must be riveting and she envied her friend. She was also full of resentment. She and Father Felix had to keep their eyes on the girls while Mrs. Johnston was wrapped up in a girl's private life. Mrs. Hopwood could only hope that Mrs. Johnston was learning something helpful and not just being a nosy parker, wasting time.

"Notice the mosaics on the upper part of the wall," Judy said, although Mrs. Hopwood was the only one who actually looked at the wall. "And leaning against the far right there are three marble tombs, containing the remains of the wife of William I, and his sons, Roger and Henry."

"How come they ain't in a cemetery?" one girl hollered out.

"Royalty was often entombed in the church or the catacombs, which we won't be visiting."

"Why not?" another girl yelled out.

"Yeah, how come?" another girl squawked.

"It's not on our tour," Judy said dryly. "And please don't lean against the brass railing."

"And what about Etna?" another girl whined. "My father said that's Sicily's main attraction. I want to see it change color."

"That's on the other side of the island. Now if you look at the top of the ceiling—" Judy pointed up about a hundred feet "—you will see a painting of four archangels. Now some of you—" she turned towards Father Felix "—may be wondering how this is so, when we all know that there were only three archangels."

"Are you wondering?" Mrs. Hopwood whispered to Father Felix, who merely glowered at her. He was doing that a lot lately, glaring at her and she was convinced that something was bothering him and it wasn't Sapphire because the glaring had begun long before Sapphire disappeared.

"Well, I'll tell you why," Judy said with much enthusiasm. "Because that angel there on the left—does everyone see him? That angel is Satan. He was originally an archangel before he fell from grace. He was a…" she paused and then said with a voice dripping with venom, "he was a traitor."

Mrs. Hopwood felt a hand on her shoulder and she let out a startled cry and a muffled curse.

All heads turned from Satan to her. She whipped around and saw Mrs. Johnston behind her. "I'm sorry," she mumbled and, because Mrs. Johnston was beckoning to her and because Mrs. Hopwood was a curious woman, she left the pew and followed Mrs. Johnston outside.

"Well," she asked the moment the church door closed.

"I think I know where Sapphire is."

"Really? How did you find out? What's in the diary? Is she all right?"

"It's very complicated and I may be wrong. I'm going to look for her. I'll meet you back at the hotel after lunch."

Mrs. Hopwood stared at her friend. Her first thought was that Mrs. Johnston was just trying to get out of her chaperone duties, her second—that if what Mrs. Johnston said was true, it could be dangerous.

"Don't you think you should wait," Mrs. Hopwood said, "and we could all go together? You and I and Father Felix. I mean, I think we should all listen to her explanation. Don't you?"

"We don't have time. I'll see you later."

And just like that Mrs. Johnston walked away. Mrs. Hopwood wondered where she was going and how she intended to get there.

The girls were pouring out of the cathedral now and it had started to rain. They were shrieking, trying to protect their blown-dry hair as they raced for the bus, leaving for Corleone.

Mrs. Hopwood couldn't say why but she had an ominous feeling as she saw Mrs. Johnston swallowed up from sight.

This had all become too complicated. Not only was it dangerous, they were thousands of miles away from home, in a foreign country, where neither one of them spoke the language. They were responsible for teenage girls, whom they didn't even know.

I shouldn't have let her go, Mrs. Hopwood thought, as she made her way to the bus.

Although how she could have prevented it, she wasn't certain.

THEY RODE UP the Madome Mountains, where the bus swirled in a zigzag, dangerously close to the cliff. Mrs. Hopwood prayed under her breath as Judy went on and on about the beautiful view, the town high above the sea, sandwiched between two valleys.

Mrs. Hopwood took out her rosary beads.

Finally the bus stopped. Mrs. Hopwood was feeling dizzy and nauseous and not at all like touring the museum. She stepped down on the uneven ground slowly, her legs still wobbling and then limped up a torturous flight of stairs.

As they lined up to go into the museum, she couldn't help but be concerned about Sapphire. Would her drug smuggling get them all in trouble? Would the Sicilian authorities think that the chaperones were somehow involved in the crime? Would Judy report them? Grim pictures of jail cells ran through her mind—she and Mrs. Johnston confined to a cell.

And what about poor Sapphire? What if something had really happened to her? What if she had been murdered and somehow the delay in reporting her missing had resulted in her death? What if they could have saved her by acting sooner? And what if they had to live with that knowledge for the rest of their lives?

"All right, girls—" Judy clapped her hands "—you're in for a treat."

"Yeah, right."

"When are we going to the wine factory? My mother said to bring home a few bottles."

"You can't buy wine—you're underage," Father Felix said.

"Not in Sicily."

Mrs. Hopwood separated from the squabbling. She didn't care what they did. She just wanted to be home with her crabby husband and her wild son.

A potbellied man was their guide and he was most animated even if the tourists weren't. He showed them pictures by the painter, Velasquez and sculptures by Lorenzo Marabitti.

"We got better art in the Met," one girl huffed.

"I got better sculptures in my backyard," another girl smirked.

They were shown stamps and coins and then a girl with green streaks in her hair raised her hand. "Isn't this the museum where that coin was stolen?"

The tour guide looked momentarily embarrassed as he fixed his lopsided horn-rimmed glasses. "It was most unfortunate." His voice held a note of doom.

"My father said someone was asleep on the job."

"If your father is referring to the night guard, he's been fired." The tour guide looked at Father Felix as if to say help, but Father Felix seemed to be studying another coin locked in a glass cubicle.

"So how was it stolen?" a girl asked as she snapped her chewing gum.

"Did you ever get it back?" asked another girl who was sipping a diet Coke.

"I'm sorry but refreshments are not allowed here." The tour guide looked frazzled and unhappy.

"No one said nothing about gum."

"I wasn't talking about your gum." He signaled for a guard who came over and stood by the soda-sipping girl.

"There's a wastepaper basket over there," the guard said. "Please be careful while disposing of your can."

"I wouldn't mess with him," Father Felix said.

"I paid good money for this," the girl sulked. "I'll meet you outside."

"You'll miss the last part of the tour and you won't be able to buy postcards," the tour guide threatened.

"Yeah, well, I'll cry myself to sleep tonight," the girl said.

"Don't go anywhere," Mrs. Hopwood shouted after her, because all she could think was that then they would have two girls missing. Although, if the truth be told she wouldn't care if they all went missing.

MRS. HOPWOOD WAS WALKING, sipping a grape soda when she stopped at a stand to admire some aprons.

"You don't even cook," Father Felix reminded her.

"My mother does and so do my sisters and I have to bring them back some souvenirs." She took a large sip of her grape juice.

The man behind the stand grimaced.

Mrs. Hopwood looked down and saw the same man in the picture she had seen last night on the television. She wished that Mrs. Johnston was there so she could confer with her. Instead Mrs. Hopwood bent down and picked up the newspaper.

"You pay before you look," the man demanded.

"Where did you get that grape juice?" Judy said from behind.

"What does it say?" Mrs. Hopwood put the paper in front of Father Felix and then changed her mind and presented it to Judy instead.

"You pay," the man repeated.

"It says...it says—" Judy stuttered, "—the print is so small."

"Give me that." Father Felix grabbed the paper.

"Is this the man Mrs. Johnston saw running out of the confessional?" Mrs. Hopwood asked Father Felix.

Father Felix scowled.

"What does it say?" Mrs. Hopwood turned her attention towards Judy and edged backwards.

"It say he criminal," the man answered. "And you pay."

While Mrs. Hopwood was searching for the right change, her hand brushed against Father Felix, who jarred her and caused Mrs. Hopwood to spill the soda all over the newspaper.

"Well, I couldn't read it anyway," she said.

"You pay," the man demanded.

"You spilled it." Mrs. Hopwood turned towards Father Felix. She shrugged and walked away.

THIRTY-THREE

SHE DIDN'T KNOW how long she was hiding in the church. And, in retrospect, it seemed like a stupid idea.

But she didn't know what else to do. She couldn't go back to the hotel. She was sure to face a firing squad, with those two teachers and that grim-looking priest. No doubt they had already called the authorities.

And then there was him. She wasn't even sure who he was. Only that if she didn't come up with the merchandise tonight, then he would be in trouble, which meant that she would be in trouble. They might even want to involve her in the setup and then the big guns would be after her, or maybe her family. And God, how long could she hide in a church?

She was done praying. She had said four rosaries and five acts of contrition and even an Apostles' Creed. But she was hungry and tired and she had to pee. She was also scared. She had spent the night alone in this creepy place, which was bad enough but now the church was opening and tourists would be pouring in and what would she do?

She looked up at the crucifix, praying for a sign, but all she heard was the sound of silence. And then the sound of keys. Sapphire fled into the street.

THIRTY-FOUR

HE WAS A PRIEST. He was a man of principle and he had to find a way to make this all right. It was all on him.

He had hoped that his face did not betray him when he saw the picture in the paper Mrs. Hopwood flung on him. Later when they got back to the hotel, he went and bought another copy (the one Mrs. Hopwood looked at was covered with grape soda) and he read it with great interest. But it gave him no more information than he already had.

The man by the name of Carlos Medina, a well-known coin collector, was suspected of robbing a coin from a museum. Although they didn't think he had been able to do this on his own, the robbers had obviously trusted him to depose of the stolen merchandise. Both he and the coin were missing and it was believed he had left the country.

Well, Father Felix knew that Medina had left the country. But the coin was still buried in Sicily.

He made up his mind about two things.

If Mrs. Johnston did not find Sapphire, they

were going to the authorities. He felt as if they were in deep enough as it was, finding the drugs and not reporting them. Of course, this would be a slur on their names, but at least he was a priest and that might count for something. He would just have to tough out the consequences.

Tomorrow was the last free day he had. After that there was only one more day of tours and they were headed home. He had to go back to the crypt by himself, somehow manage to stay locked in there and then find out whether or not the coin was buried beneath that body. Again, another tough situation but, then again, life was full of tough situations.

Father Felix made all these decisions as he got off the bus in front of the hotel. And then he saw Sapphire.

AT FIRST HE DIDN'T recognize her. She looked disheveled as though she hadn't slept at all which, of course, she probably hadn't. At first he wasn't sure if it was really her, but then the girl met his eyes and he read terror. Then she started to run away.

He wasn't a fast runner, in spite of his intention to join a gym and cycle and walk on the treadmill and pretend to climb stairs and do all those other things, but supervising a school took most of his energy. And even if he could catch up with her, it would mean knocking over tourists, who were meandering in the narrow street.

Instead he called to Mrs. Hopwood who had stopped at an outside vendor and was holding a set of bangle bracelets.

She looked up, annoyed.

"Sapphire," he screamed as Sapphire ran towards her.

Mrs. Hopwood dropped the bracelet on the concrete and Father Felix heard the vendor curse in Sicilian. But Mrs. Hopwood didn't understand Sicilian so she wasn't bothered (and perhaps she wouldn't be bothered even if she did understand). She just reached out and grabbed Sapphire by her dirty T-shirt and then Sapphire began to curse. And Mrs. Hopwood cursed right back.

"Where have you been, damn it all?"

Sapphire stood rooted to the spot, looking vacant, sweat running down her swollen and bloated face. He noticed the deep circles under her eyes. "You're not my mother," she finally said, her expression stony.

"No, but we are your chaperones and we're supposed to keep track of you."

"Who says?"

She was bold and Father Felix hated bold. "Sapphire, we found the drugs."

She shrugged. "So what are you going to do, put me in a Sicilian jail?"

She was tough but Father Felix was used to tough. "We have to talk," was all he said.

"Do you have any idea about how much inconvenience you have caused us?" Mrs. Hopwood was looking at the bracelets, which were now back on the card table, and then to the face of the vendor, angry and daring. "Poor Mrs. Johnston went to find you."

"Where did she think I was?" her voice was husky.

Father Felix and Mrs. Hopwood looked at each other, neither saying a word. Father Felix was not about to admit that Mrs. Johnston had read Sapphire's diary. He knew that was the ultimate transgression—even more serious than disappearing for a night or bringing drugs into the country.

"I don't think you understand how much trouble you're in," Mrs. Hopwood said.

"No, I don't think *you* understand." Her voice was bitter. "You took my drugs and there are people looking for those drugs. I'm not the only one who is going to be in big trouble because I didn't deliver." Sapphire squinted her eyes and stared at Mrs. Hopwood.

"I didn't take the drugs," Mrs. Hopwood croaked

Father Felix was going to pipe in also, but then thought that sounded cowardly. Besides, he wasn't even sure of what was to be done now.

"You and I—" he turned towards Sapphire, who was still managing to look sullen and angry, as though they had created the problem "—and Mrs. Hopwood and Mrs. Johnston are going to sit down and find a way out of this mess. And if you attempt to run again, then I will have every Sicilian police officer looking for you. Do you understand?"

Father Felix might have taken pity on her, if she had looked scared. But instead she just looked tired and worn out. "I get it," she said.

"Good, now let's go inside."

As Father Felix sat down, he felt a little victorious. All right, he hadn't really solved the problem, but at least he managed to take the rudder. While it was true that he wasn't at St. Polycarp, and technically he had no control over Mrs. Hopwood and Mrs. Johnston, there was a certain amount of responsibility that came with the collar. Also, he was a man and it was expected.

But he also knew that it was easier to be a leader when dealing with Mrs. Hopwood. Mrs. Johnston was an entirely different matter.

Mrs. Hopwood sat beside him. "So," she said

in a challenging voice, "what are we going to do now?"

He had no idea.

THIRTY-FIVE

MRS. HOPWOOD DECIDED to put the entire matter into Amelia Johnston's capable hands. She couldn't wait to return to her room. She and Amelia and Father Felix would sit in the café across the street—even if they had to pay extra euros just to have a seat—and decide on the course of action.

But when Mrs. Hopwood arrived in her room, she received the shock of her life.

MRS. JOHNSTON WASN'T THERE. At first Mrs. Hopwood didn't think much of it, she merely assumed that Amelia hadn't come back. Until she went into the bathroom and she found that some of her things were gone, the important things, like her toothbrush and her toothpaste. She ran to the closet and opened it. Mrs. Johnston's clothes were also missing.

And then Mrs. Hopwood noticed the note on the desk.

Her heart was beating so wildly, she thought she might be having a heart attack. She grabbed the paper and sank down on Mrs. Johnston's bed, too frightened to read it. She thought maybe she should call Father Felix and together they could go over the letter—which she was fairly certain was a ransom note.

But would kidnappers have allowed Mrs. Johnston to take her toothbrush?

Dear Julia—
I am so sorry.

I just received notice that the penny Jeffrey swallowed is now lodged in his intestines. It is blocking his liver, which as we know, is a major organ. He has been rushed to the hospital for emergency surgery. He is crying for his mother.

I have to go.

I know that I am leaving you in the lurch and I feel terrible about it. Especially since there is that horrible problem. By the way, I am going to leave the deodorant bottles in your suitcase.

But think of it this way. Father Felix is more than competent and it's only for three more days.

I would have given anything for this not to have happened, believe me. I hope to get a flight out tonight.

I'll see you in the States.

Mrs. Hopwood read the note over three times, each time having a different reaction. Her first reaction was pity for Amelia and her husband, and especially little Jeffrey, who had to endure surgery. Her second reaction was anger. She didn't blame Amelia for leaving. Mrs. Hopwood was also a mother and if anything happened to Alexander, she wouldn't hesitate to leave all those giggling girls behind and board the next plane home. The person she blamed was Peter for allowing Jeffrey to swallow the penny—why wasn't he watching his son, instead of some sports program on television—and finally she put the blame squarely on Jeffrey's shoulders. He was four years old. Mrs. Hopwood was certain that his mother had told him over and over again to keep things out of his mouth. But he was a rebellious child, a mischievous child, and now look at all the havoc he caused. Mrs. Hopwood doubted very much if Jeffrey had learned his lesson. Her third reaction was one of panic. It would be bad enough if Amelia left before the trip was up. She and Father Felix would have to divide the chaperoning duties between them, not to speak of the fact that Mrs. Hopwood would miss Amelia's company.

But there was the matter of the drugs, that entire mess that she and Father Felix would now have to sort out, while Mrs. Johnston was thousands of miles away in a hospital, sitting by her son's bedside.

Well, there was nothing to be done. Except tell Father Felix who would not be happy. Mrs. Hopwood went over to her suitcase and began to rifle through it. She couldn't find the bottles of deodorant. She took everything out. Nothing.

She read the note over just to be certain and then began to search the room. Mrs. Johnston must have forgotten to take the bottles out of her own suitcase instead. Great. Mrs. Hopwood could not imagine how this was going to end, except to say, probably badly.

THIRTY-SIX

SAPPHIRE KNOCKED ON the door to room 213, fear fluttering in her chest. It was important that she act cool, not let them see how frightened she really was. Those uptight chaperones were just looking to punish her because she was young and pretty. It occurred to her that maybe, just maybe she could get them to take pity on her, if she told them the real reason she had agreed to smuggle drugs. Maybe she could even shed a few tears.

There was no doubt in her mind that one of the chaperones had taken her diary. So maybe they already knew. At first Sapphire had accused Therese, who denied the accusation vehemently. Sapphire had quickly backed down because it was apparent that her roommate was doing everything in her power to distance herself from Sapphire. She was petrified of knowing too much,

But not those chaperones. They had definitely snooped and they thought nothing of invading her privacy. Wasn't that stealing? Weren't they breaking the law?

The priest answered the door, grim and somber. Sapphire didn't know why he was looking so serious. Certainly he had heard plenty of confessions, robberies, adulteries, even murders. What was a little grass flown across a plane?

He held the door open and she noticed right away that the heavyset teacher was missing. Only the colorfully dressed one was present and she was wringing her hands, walking back and forth in turquoise spikes, looking stressed and worried.

"Where's the other chaperone?" Sapphire asked to no one in particular.

"We don't have to answer your questions," Father Felix snapped. "We have questions of our own."

She shrugged, trying her best to look as blank and as still as one of those stone pillars she had seen in a crumbling cathedral.

"Sit down." The priest grabbed the desk chair and placed it in the middle of the room. Sitting down, when the two of them were standing over her would surely place Sapphire in an inferior position.

But she was probably already in an inferior position.

She exhaled and plunked down, clenching her fists.

"Well," Father Felix bellowed, "we are waiting for an explanation."

Sapphire remained mute.

"Are you a drug addict?" Mrs. Hopwood asked tensely.

"No!"

"So you planned on selling the drugs?" Father Felix asked.

Sapphire thought it best not to respond. Evidently they had not yet read her diary.

"Maybe you have a boyfriend who persuaded you to do this crazy thing," Mrs. Hopwood said in a rather sympathetic voice.

"No. No boyfriend. Besides, marijuana is not a hard drug. It's already legal in fourteen states."

"That's only for medicinal purpose," Father Felix snapped. "Why did you agree to do such a stupid thing?"

"I needed the money," Sapphire said simply.

"Because you're a drug addict," Father Felix burst out.

Sapphire's only response was to sniffle disgustedly.

"This isn't going anywhere," Mrs. Hopwood stated the obvious. "Sapphire, listen, we want to help you. Really we do. If you are in trouble…"

"I am in trouble," Sapphire leaped up, "and, if you want to help me, you'll do what I say. You don't know these people. They're dangerous. When I don't show up with the goods tonight, they're going to want to know what happened to that marijuana. If they think that I've been caught and you have the bottles, we're all going to be in trouble. If you would just give the bottles back to me…"

Sapphire did not miss the frightened look that passed between the priest and the woman.

"We can't do that," Father Felix said.

And then Sapphire understood. "You don't have the bottles, do you? You turned it over to the police. Then why aren't the police here, arresting me? Or maybe you intervened on my behalf, and maybe now you think everything is going to be hunky-dory and I owe you big time, but you don't know the terrible trouble I could be in!" A few tears leaked from her eyes and she wiped them away with her sleeve.

"If you're in trouble, you have no one to blame but yourself," Father Felix said, without one bit of empathy in his voice. "You not only put yourself in danger but you put me and Mrs. Hopwood and Mrs. Johnston in danger as well, not to speak of all the other girls who came to Sicily to have a good time. In addition, you have blackened all of our names."

He had to be kidding, Sapphire thought. Blackened their names—a continent away? "You're not being very nice to me," she grumbled.

Father Felix and Mrs. Hopwood exchanged exasperated looks, which Sapphire caught at once. She had won.

"Go back to your room for now," Father Felix ordered. "If I catch you running away again…"

"I'm not going anyplace," Sapphire said in a weary voice.

"Or any attempt to meet this drug dealer, you will be sitting in a cell in ten minutes flat. Do I make myself clear?"

Sapphire did her best to look petulant.

"Do I make myself clear?" he bellowed.

"Yeah, I get it. Oh by the way," she said as she rose, "Could I have my diary back?"

Again they looked at each other, confused and scared. They didn't have her diary or the drugs. And it was difficult to determine what could get her in more trouble.

She left then and she was tempted to put her ear to the door, just to see what they were saying, or what they were going to do next.

It didn't matter. Without the drugs, they had no proof at all that she had been doing anything. She could always say that she brought along a lot of deodorant and the chaperones had caused trouble just to be mean. They might not believe Sapphire—after all it was her word against a priest's but, on the other hand, she could hardly be arrested with such flimsy evidence.

Unless they brought out the diary. But she could always claim she was working on a short story. Teachers believed shit like that—they thought every kid liked to write.

Besides, if all the priest was concerned about was his blackened name, then there was a very good chance he was just going to drop the matter. Of course, he could make life difficult for her in the upcoming days. The upcoming three days.

All she had to do now was to evade the man who she was supposed to meet and she'd be home safe. Except there was no safety there, either.

THIRTY-SEVEN

FATHER FELIX COULD not sleep. His dreams were confusing and disturbing, no doubt caused by the bizarre and grotesque figures he saw at the Villa Palagonia. He woke repeatedly, panicky, with a tightness engulfing him.

Two matters weighed heavily on his mind. One of them was the situation with Sapphire. He was unsure of what to do and Mrs. Hopwood, as usual, wasn't very helpful. One thing they both agreed on—without the bottles it would be impossible to charge or convict Sapphire.

Not that either one of them wanted to do that. He felt bad for Sapphire. She had a certain desperation about her. He had often seen it in his students at St. Polycarp. Their home lives forced them to break the law, to do unthinkable things. They felt trapped with no way out. He tried to provide a safe haven for them during the day, tried to install morals and hope into them, tried to teach them to trust God. He prayed for them—prayed that before they walked down that road where there was no turning back, they would make a different choice.

Sometimes he succeeded. Sometimes the kid ended up in jail or on a slab in the funeral parlor.

He wanted to give Sapphire that chance.

Then there was the matter of the missing drugs. If Mrs. Johnston had taken the bottles by mistake. What if she got stopped at the airport?

It hadn't happened. If it had, she would have been back here lickity-split. Still he didn't feel good, letting the matter ride. He was supposed to help Sapphire and, if she had the drugs, she had to be persuaded to give them back, not to go through with the trade. The trade was supposed to have happened last night. Was Sapphire in some sort of danger now? And if she was, did that fall on him because he hadn't gone to the Sicilian police?

And then there was the matter of the crypt. He had already decided how he was going to handle this. Tomorrow night after dinner, he was going to go by himself. On Wednesday evenings the catacombs were open until eight o'clock. He would remain behind and investigate. Hopefully, he could just sneak out afterwards. It wasn't perfect but he could think of no other way.

His head ached and his stomach cramped. He longed to be back at St. Polycarp, in his own nice office, which faced the park, his world where he was in charge, where the first-grade students to the eighth-grade pupils respected and listened to him, where he had power, where things were simple and he could yell and people listened to him.

He was just drifting off, thinking about September bulletin boards when there was a loud rap on the door. He stayed motionless. Up until now, he hadn't taken Sapphire's threats seriously but maybe she was right. Maybe the drugs were connected to the Mafia—after all this was Sicily—and a thug was waiting on the other side of the door with a machine gun because Sapphire hadn't shown up.

The rap was louder. Perhaps he should find his collar. The fact the he was a priest might help. Maybe they would just shoot him in the head instead of torturing him.

Someone rattled the knob. They could break the door down and that's just what they would have to do because he certainly wasn't going to open it. He reached for the telephone to call for help, dropping his travel alarm clock on the floor, where it fell with a loud thud.

"Father Felix, wake up!"

It was Mrs. Hopwood. He was going to kill her. He picked up the alarm clock. What could she possibly want at two in the morning?

"I have to talk to you. It's important!"

Maybe she wasn't alone. Maybe they had gotten to her first.

"Please!"

"What is this about?" he asked with great caution.

"I can't discuss it in the hall. Please open the door."

Father Felix knew a dangerous situation when he was confronted with one. "No."

"What do you mean, no?" She was clearly getting hysterical, drawing attention to herself. While this wasn't unusual for Mrs. Hopwood—who could become hysterical over a ladybug—he doubted that, if someone had a gun to her head, the criminal would allow her to cause a scene and wake the other tourists.

"Not unless you tell me what this is about," he said a bit more firmly.

"It's about Mrs. Johnston."

"Are you alone?"

"Of course I'm alone. Let me in!"

Still he wasn't sure. So he opened the door, just a crack, pushing his full weight against it. Just in case. But there stood Mrs. Hopwood in a robe striped with every imaginable color, and some that weren't so imaginable, and wearing a neon-pink nightgown underneath it and looking quite vexed.

He opened the door a little bit wider and she scurried in and slammed it behind her, switching on the overhead light. He blinked several times and then remembered that he was in a T-shirt and rather worn pajama bottoms, not very priestlike, but she didn't seem to notice.

"Something horrible has happened!"

He knew Mrs. Hopwood well and something horrible could be a broken heel or a scuffed patent-leather shoe, but in light of all that had happened..."

Father Felix released a low groan. "It's two o'clock in the morning and I'm really tired. Could you please get to the point?"

"I was tossing and turning—my room is very spooky, you know, because it faces the alley and then I noticed that Mrs. Johnston's drawer was slightly open. It looked ominous—" Mrs. Hopwood was telling the tale, embellishing it, no doubt, the way she did when reading Bible stories to her second graders, with too much drama and too much enthusiasm, "so I got up to see for myself what was blocking the drawer. And would you like to see what I found?"

"The deodorant bottles. And couldn't this have waited until morning?"

"No," Mrs. Hopwood said, victorious, "not the deodorant bottles." She dug into her robe of many colors and pulled out a small square leather case.

"What is it?"

"It's Mrs. Johnston's passport."

"She forgot her passport?"

"She did."

He shook his head and sunk on to the bed. She sunk beside him. He didn't think it was right, him half dressed, and her here in the middle of the night. Not that anyone knew but still appearances.

"You don't get it, do you?"

He stared at her blankly.

"She could not have gotten on the plane without her passport."

"So she didn't go home."

"She didn't go home."

"Then," he paused, "where is she?"

Mrs. Hopwood leaped up. "That's the question, where is she?"

He couldn't think of a plausible answer but he didn't have to because it seemed as if Mrs. Hopwood had several theories of her own. "I'll tell you what I think. I think she has been kidnapped!"

"Kidnapped?"

"That's right, kidnapped. You heard what Sapphire said. These people are dangerous."

He reached for his robe. "You're not making any sense," he said irritably. "If they were after drugs, all she had to do was give them the bottles. And really it was just a little marijuana. I'm not saying what Sapphire did wasn't wrong and wasn't illegal but I hardly think that the Mafia is going to kidnap a lone school teacher…" He wasn't about to admit that he was thinking just the opposite seconds ago.

"Where could she go without her passport?"

"I'm not sure." He could at least put his robe on because something told him that Mrs. Hopwood wasn't going anywhere soon. "But look, we know that the penny Jeffrey swallowed traveled to his intestines—"

"We know no such thing."

"Didn't you read the note?"

Mrs. Hopwood reluctantly nodded.

"You must know Amelia's handwriting by now. Was it written in her handwriting?" Again, Mrs. Hopwood nodded but then quickly added, "But they could have coerced her into writing it."

"Then they would have had to know about Jeffrey and the penny. And I'm sure that Amelia spoke to Peter—"

"They could have grabbed her on the way to the airport."

He threw his hands up in the air. "I got to tell you, I don't see it. Look, let's be reasonable. Amelia is a formable woman."

"Not when she is up against drug dealers and kidnappers!"

He drew a deep breath, trying to control his temper. "Maybe she had two passports. Did you ever think of that? Maybe she thought she lost the first one and then applied for another, then found the first one and kept them both."

Mrs. Hopwood was shaking her head in the most annoying way. "She would have told me. She told me everything and she never mentioned such a thing. She tells me things I don't want to know. Personal things about her and Peter. Since the twins have been born."

Now it was he who shook his head. "Look, Amelia left hours ago. If she's not home by now, then, at the very least, she's talked to Peter en route. If she hasn't arrived, or if she hasn't called him on her cell, then I'm sure that he'd phone the hotel to find out what happened to her. And I'm certain the management in the hotel would inform us and since we haven't heard anything…"

"Her cell," Mrs. Hopwood repeated thoughtfully, "her cell. Don't you see—" her voice was now taking on that excited quality which scared the hell out of him "—she didn't have her cell. Don't you remember it was stolen?"

"Yeah."

"He couldn't have reached her on her cell to tell her about Jeffrey!"

"So what? Maybe he called the hotel and got the message to her that way. What difference does it make? She obviously spoke to him or she wouldn't just leave Sicily and fly thousands of miles home."

"Maybe not. Maybe it was just a whole made-up story."

He was thinking maybe, just maybe, of moving Mrs. Hopwood up from the second grade to the fourth grade. Now he realized that it was be a major mistake. She was best with seven-year-old children. Her ability for logical thinking was severely impaired.

"And how would these kidnappers know about the penny stuck somewhere in Jeffrey?" he continued.

Mrs. Hopwood was mute. For a moment. "I still would feel much better if we called him."

"It's two o'clock in the morning!"

"Not in New York. It's only eight at night."

"And what are we going to say? We just called to find out whether or not your wife has been kid napped?"

Mrs. Hopwood glared at him with grave suspicion in her eyes. For a moment he was certain that she thought he had something to do with Amelia's disappearance. "Of course not. We could call just to make sure she got home all right. We could ask about Jeffrey. That's reasonable, isn't it? We're her friends. If her son is in intensive care, wouldn't we want to know?"

"Okay, we'll call first thing in the morning." She glared at him again. "The phone place across the street is closed at this hour."

"First thing in the morning it will be the middle of the night in New York. Besides, you have a phone card. I saw you use it. You were calling someone." Again the suspicion in her voice. "I don't know who."

"My mother! I was calling my mother! I am allowed to call my mother."

"The only person I want you to call right now is Peter."

He knew when he was licked. "I'll meet you downstairs in ten minutes." Again the dirty look. "I am not going down half-dressed and if I were you, I'd put something decent on."

"I am decent," she protested, "just very worried."

"THERE IS NO ANSWER," he clunked down the phone.

"You didn't leave a message." She shot him a look of annoyance.

"The machine didn't pick up." He headed for the elevator.

"That doesn't make sense." She actually pulled him by the shoulder and whirled him around. "They always have the machine on, unless Peter is on the computer, and why would Peter by on the computer if Jeffrey is in intensive care and his wife is on her way home."

"Because maybe, just maybe—" he jabbed the up button "—Jeffrey is out of intensive care and Amelia is already there and they're all at the hospital."

The elevator doors snapped open and they both got in.

"Are you sure you dialed the right number?" she asked.

He shook his head. "Of course I dialed the right number," he said in a weary voice, because by this time he was exhausted and felt as though he were sleepwalking. "I have been dialing Amelia Johnston's number for years now."

"But there were all those international codes."

He wasn't even going to dignify that concern with a response.

"Well, I'm going to call again tomorrow," she said, as though it were a threat.

The elevator stopped and the door opened on their floor. "Look," he said, "I don't want you to take this the wrong way, but I don't think I'll be going on any more international trips with you or Mrs. Johnston."

That stare again. "And what makes you think

that either Amelia or I want to go on any more international trips with you?" With that remark, she stormed down the hall and into her room.

THIRTY-EIGHT

THIS WAS A PERFECT opportunity to search the priest's room. Sapphire saw him leave with that skinny chaperone.

And Sapphire had learned a long time ago how easy it was to pick a lock. And this Sicilian lock—a piece of cake.

The room was really orderly—but then again the man was a priest and Sapphire had always thought they were neat freaks. So it was easy to search, and how many places could he have hidden six deodorant push-up sticks?

And her diary.

She looked in the closet, the medicine cabinet, his suitcase, under his boxer shorts and lavender-smelling socks, even behind the bed. She put her hand beneath the mattress and only came up with mouse turds.

Nice.

She opened the desk drawer and found nothing but a copy of the Bible, his personal Bible, engraved just for him. She opened it out of curiosity and found a piece of paper stuck in one of the pages.

On the paper was a number, just a single number. #772.

Goose bumps ran down her bare arms. That was the same number that she found in the compact in the alley. Something was going on. Maybe this man wasn't a priest at all, but an escaped criminal and the two teachers were part of his posse.

No on second thought, they acted too much like teachers. They had to be blissfully unaware.

Well, maybe just maybe, this magic number would come in handy. She could use it for leverage to get back what rightfully belonged to her.

She peeked out the door and closed it behind her.

It didn't lock, of course, but who cared? He wouldn't be able to prove anything and if he did— she did have that magic number.

THIRTY-NINE

AMELIA JOHNSTON HAD never been so scared in her life.

She had grown up in an inner-city neighborhood, where walking down the street after dark was dangerous. But yet she managed to stand up to gang members who were trying to recruit her younger brother—now a successful lawyer. She made friends with the vicious and mean girls in her school and she was able to balance on the tightrope between being a geek and being the kind of girl no one wanted to mess with. Her first job was teaching in a high school where the kids would slash your tires if you gave them a cross look.

Her tires were never slashed and she managed to gain their respect.

Never had she been this scared—not when she was in labor with two wiggling boys, each weighing well over seven pounds, not when she thought Peter might leave her for another woman (and all the time he was planning a surprise birthday party) and not when her father had the stroke and lay dying in a hospital bed. Because now she realized that she had mere hours to live.

She didn't understand what happened, could barely make sense of it. She had finished reading Sapphire's diary, which by itself, was most eye-opening. It turned out that the girl had a sad life with an abusive stepfather, who had a thing for Sapphire's younger sister. Sapphire wanted to get some money to bring her sister to some relatives out of state. And whenever she felt at the end of her rope, she would hide in a church.

Mrs. Johnston returned to the hotel with the intention of obtaining a map, hoping to locate the nearest churches. Instead when she went to the front desk with her request, she learned that there was a note from Peter. He called to say that the penny Jeffrey had swallowed had migrated to his intestines and immediate surgery was warranted. Jeffrey was hollering for his mother.

And Amelia knew that was where she belonged. She didn't hesitate. She packed her bags. She meant to leave Sapphire's diary for Julia and the deodorant bottles. But in her haste she did neither. Nor did she call Peter back. She had planned to do that once she reached the airport.

That was a mistake, a mistake which now might cost her her life. She still couldn't figure it out. How did they know about Jeffrey? But they must have known. Because the moment she stepped out of the hotel, there was a taxi right out front waiting for her. It was like a miracle because the desk clerk said that the cab he called wouldn't be there for another twenty minutes. And she wouldn't have gotten into the cab if the driver hadn't come out and, in a thick Sicilian accent, called her by name. She was so upset by the thought that something had happened to her little boy that she wasn't thinking clearly.

She got into the cab. She didn't know the neighborhood so she had no idea of where the man was taking her. On the highway, certainly, she remembered a lot of highways when she first boarded the bus from the airport with Mrs. Hopwood and Father Felix. The little towns whizzed by but then they had marveled at the scenery.

Amelia was not marveling at anything now. They seemed to be driving for a long time. Still she did not think that was peculiar. Until they entered into what looked like a forest. This was definitely not a place she passed on arriving in Sicily. She would have remembered it. Perhaps the driver was lost.

"Excuse me," she said in her seventh-grade-teacher voice, "but you were supposed to be taking me to the airport." He stared at her with black beady eyes through the rearview mirror. A peculiar looking man—he seemed vaguely familiar. He had bushy gray hair, a long, thin nose, not unlike a sewing needle. She looked down at the back of the seat, hoping to learn his name or at least be reassured that he had a legitimate cab license. There was nothing.

"Is this a shortcut?" she asked in a hopeful voice.

"Shut up!"

At first she could not believe that he was speaking to her. She couldn't imagine what she had done to warrant such rudeness. Perhaps he was talking into a cell phone, a wireless device.

"Sir, where are you taking me?"

"I said shut the hell up!"

He *was* talking to her and something was very wrong. She had once seen this movie where locals kidnapped wealthy tourists and took everything they possessed. That was fine with her. They could have it all. Just let her go home to her husband and her babies.

She looked at the doors and noticed that they were locked. Maybe she could open them from the inside, but so what? Where would she go in the middle of the woods? Her best bet was to be quiet and respectful. And to pray.

And then it occurred to her that this was not an accident. They were purposely kidnapping her.

The man had called her by name. The hotel must have told him. Then she thought about the drugs and realized that maybe the hotel was somehow in cohorts with Sapphire, and God it was all so confusing.

Up ahead she saw a small hut. Oh my God, she thought, is this where he's taking me? Why?

He stopped the car with a lurch. She remained motionless as he flung open the door. "Get out!"

She stared at him for a few seconds, fear and panic clouding her thoughts. It was a few seconds too long because he grabbed her by her sweater and pulled her. "If it's the marijuana you want," she said desperately, "it's in my suitcase. I shouldn't have taken it with me. I should have left it with Mrs. Hopwood." Maybe it was wrong to involve Mrs. Hopwood, but she didn't know what else to do. "But I was so worried about my son that I forgot to take it out. He's all right, isn't he? My son, I mean?"

He didn't answer her, just pushed her ahead into the hut. He's going to rape me, she thought, and again she wondered why. Why not go after Mrs. Hopwood who flaunted her curves in all those spandex outfits and all those high-heel shoes and all that cleavage. There was nothing inside the hut but a chair and a table and a cot.

"Please, don't hurt me," she begged. "I'm a

mother. My son—do you know—I mean, he's supposed to be in intensive care. Do you know anything about that?"

He stared at her. "There is only one thing I want to know about, lady. Where the hell is that coin?"

At first she thought that she misunderstood him and in a soft, polite voice said, "Pardon?"

Her politeness seemed to enrage him. "The coin, lady! The coin!"

"I think you have me mixed up with someone else. I don't know anything at all about a coin. Nothing. Honestly. If I did, don't you think…"

"Listen, don't play with me. As tough as you think you are, I guarantee you're no match for me and wait, just wait, until you meet my associates, which you will do. As soon as it gets dark, you and me, we're going to the crypts."

"The crypts…"

"Now, it's all coming back to you—"

"No, no, no. I've never been to the crypts. I never wanted to go to the crypts. When Mrs. Hopwood—" again she felt bad mentioning her friend's name, but after all she was only telling the truth, and Mrs. Hopwood did know something about the coin and would be in a position to put a stop to this madness "—and Father Felix asked me to go, I said straight out, absolutely not. The whole idea is so creepy…"

"Is that so?" For a moment he sounded dubious.

"Yes, that is so."

"I don't believe a word you're saying."

Her thoughts buzzed in her head, frantically and fruitlessly, like a fly trapped under a sheet of glass. "What can I do to convince you?" she blurted out.

"Nothing, nothing at all. You see, you have to know where that coin is buried because if you don't, well, let's put it this way, if you don't, you are no good to us at all."

Mrs. Johnston felt her stomach plunge down to her knees. He didn't complete the statement. He didn't have to. She knew what it was. If she found the coin—assuming that such a thing was possible—then she was still no good to him at all. Either way she was dead.

"I'll be back when it's dark," he said. "Don't even bother to escape. You will find that the windows are boarded and the door is double locked. You can scream all you want. No one will hear you." And with that chilling statement, he left.

After about ten minutes of frustration, Mrs. Johnston realized that he was right. There was no way out of the hut and somehow screaming would only waste her voice.

But she had to find a way to survive. She could buy time pretending to look for the coin in the crypt, but she wouldn't find it and it probably wouldn't matter if she did. The worst part was that no one knew that she was missing. Mrs. Hopwood would just think she went home. Peter would think she was still in Sicily. And Father Felix wouldn't give the matter a second thought.

I have to survive, she thought, *for my little boys. I can't have them growing up without a mother and I will not be murdered in a foreign country over a matter I know nothing of. I have to think of a way to escape. I have to have a plan.* But right now, Mrs. Johnston could only find the strength to do something she hadn't done since third grade. She put her head down and wept.

FORTY

"PETER, HI, THIS IS Julia Hopwood."

"Oh, Julia." He sounded upbeat. "How are you?"

"I'm fine, just fine. Look, I know that it's early in the morning…"

"That's all right. The twins have been up since dawn."

"He's home, then?"

"Pardon?"

"Jeffrey." Mrs. Hopwood did not like the silence which followed. "The penny came out."

"Yeah, about two days after it went in."

Mrs. Hopwood watched as the streets of Sicily swirled in front of her. "He was never in the hospital?"

"The hospital?"

Don't panic him, Mrs. Hopwood thought, *and don't let him hear the panic in your voice.* "Somehow Amelia got the idea that Jeffrey was in the hospital crying for her."

"I don't understand."

"She may be on her way home."

"What's going on?"

"I don't know," Mrs. Hopwood answered honestly, "I really don't know. And as soon as I do, I'll call you. I promise." She hung up the pay phone before he could say another word.

Father Felix was sitting on the bench, enjoying a gelato.

She sank down beside him. Uneasiness tightened at the bottom of her stomach. "Amelia never made it home."

"What?" he gulped.

"Jeffrey was never in the hospital, and Peter has no idea why Amelia would think that he was."

"Are you making this up?" he accused her.

"And why would I do that?" He didn't want to be bothered. She could see that and it infuriated her. "Did you hear me? Amelia is missing. I was right on the money. She has been kidnapped and I think we should go right to the Sicilian police."

"I'm not so sure." He seemed to be watching some of the girls, running around the fountain at the Piazza Pretoria, laughing like maniacs.

She rose up in anger. "So don't come with me," she threatened. "And when the police ask me why, I will have no alternative but to tell them that I strongly suspect you have your own motives."

He yanked her back down on the bench where she fell hard.

"Did it ever occur to you that she doesn't want to be found?" Father Felix asked.

She stared at him in disbelief.

"Amelia was always talking about how she wanted to leave home, how she wanted to start a new life. She even mentioned it on this trip. You must have noticed how grumpy she was, how out-of-sorts. I think she was planning this for some time."

"You can't be serious."

From the look in his eyes, Mrs. Hopwood knew that he was.

"She would never do such a thing!" Mrs. Hopwood was adamant. "Yes, it's true, she was always making jokes about checking out, but she never meant anything by it. It was just venting, that's all. She loved her boys and her husband, she loved her job and us."

"That may be true, maybe. But sometimes you think you know someone and…"

"And you don't know them at all." Mrs. Hopwood finished the statement for him but she wasn't thinking of Amelia Johnston when she said it.

Father Felix shook his head. "I still can't imagine how the kidnappers would have known about the penny."

"You're serious, aren't you? I'll tell you how. Maybe someone overheard us and repeated it.

Someone like her…" Mrs. Hopwood saw Sapphire come out from a café and light a cigarette. She jumped up and confronted her.

"You!"

"There is nothing that says I can't smoke."

"This isn't about your cigarette. Where is she?"

Sapphire was a great actress, but then Mrs. Hopwood had already known that. "Where is who?"

"Mrs. Johnston."

"Who is Mrs. Johnston?"

Father Felix was suddenly beside Mrs. Hopwood and somehow she knew that he wasn't going to be helpful.

"You know very well who Mrs. Johnston is," she said viciously. "She is the other chaperone."

"Why would I know where she is?" Sapphire shrugged her shoulders.

"Because she has been kidnapped." Fury broke out from her, scorching her inside.

"Kidnapped!" One of the girls standing behind Sapphire exclaimed as she nudged her friend whose eyes popped out.

"Someone has been kidnapped?" Another girl who was chewing on a piece of taffy asked.

"Who has been kidnapped?" Now it was Therese's turn.

"Mrs. Hopwood, please!" Father Felix was pleading with her. "You're causing a panic here."

Mrs. Hopwood paid him no mind. "We intend to go to the police," she told Sapphire, "and tell them everything."

"But that's crazy. I don't know anything about Mrs. Johnston's disappearance. Maybe it was just a random act."

"It was not a random act. It was carefully planned out and executed by someone who knew her."

"But I didn't even know who she was," Sapphire protested.

Mrs. Hopwood felt someone tugging hard on her cardigan sweater. Father Felix dragged her over behind the church of Santa Caterina. She looked into his furious eyes, but that was all right because she was quite furious herself.

"Would you please get a hold of yourself? You are causing a scene. Just look at the circle. Strangers…" He turned towards Judy, who was suddenly by his side.

"I don't care!" And she didn't.

"You may not but…" Judy was gazing at the floor in obvious embarrassment.

"Is this about your reputation?" she asked, "and the reputation of this tour because I have to tell you—"

"Listen for a minute." Judy looked quickly at Father Felix and then looked away. "Maybe your friend just decided to take a time out—you know it happens sometimes."

"Don't even suggest that!"

"But kidnapped," Judy whispered, "I mean, who would want to kidnap her—and for what reason?"

There was a reason but Mrs. Hopwood was not about to tell Judy. And obviously neither was Father Felix, who couldn't even look at Judy.

"Okay," Judy sighed. "I understand you want to know what happened to your friend. I'm not telling you that you shouldn't pursue it. But all this hysteria won't help."

"Judy's right," Father Felix quickly echoed.

It was the united agreement that irritated Mrs. Hopwood. After all Judy didn't know Mrs. Johnston and right now she was just trying to avoid a lawsuit.

"I'll go to the police with you," Father Felix said, "but for now our best bet is to keep this quiet."

Mrs. Hopwood wasn't sure if he was right or even if he had an ulterior motive. But she doubted very much she could find her friend alone—even if she were brave enough to try.

"Okay?" he asked.

She nodded and walked towards the elevator.

He didn't say what they both knew.

It might already be too late.

FORTY-ONE

WHERE WAS HE taking her now? He hadn't even bothered to cover her eyes. And Mrs. Johnston knew why. He didn't care one bit if she saw their final destination. Because he wasn't worried whether or not she would tell anyone since she wasn't coming back.

She was so scared that she was afraid that she was going to pee, which she had to do really badly. She hadn't dared ask them if she could use the bathroom. She was terrified that they would shoot her. She should have gone in the hut but there wasn't even a pot there, and now it was too late. Too late for everything.

She wasn't going to cry. She had done enough of that already and it hadn't helped her any. On the contrary, it only made her more panicked. You have to survive, she told herself. You have two little boys who are depending on you. You have to find a way out of this situation. She repeated a mantra she had learned so long ago, "For every locked door there is a key to open it. You, simply, must find that a key."

He wanted something from her, or at least, he thought that she knew the whereabouts of some-thing important. The best thing to do was to play along and pretend that she did. That way he would think that she was of some use to him.

Never mind that she had no idea what he was talking about.

It seemed as though they had been riding for-ever when the car stopped suddenly. The car door opened and the tall, thin man ordered her to get out.

Mrs. Johnston looked around frantically, hop-ing for some sort of escape. There was nothing. A large non-descript building loomed in front of her. It looked like some sort of schoolhouse. Maybe there would be other men in the building, men who would help her. Men who would kill her. She stood there, fear rippling through her, hoping that she didn't pee, or throw up, or faint.

"Get going." He shoved her then towards the building while he fumbled around with a key in the dark. Mrs. Johnston thought he was probably trying to turn off the alarm.

Was this some sort of museum?

This time the man didn't speak only threw her indoors. The first thing she noticed was that the temperature was ice-cold and she wasn't dressed for it. Why would she be? She thought she was going to the airport. She bit her lip to stop herself from crying.

Then she looked straight ahead and saw a skeleton hanging on a hook, a skeleton with a hole in his head and a mouth open in a silent scream. Mrs. Johnston knew exactly where she was. She was in the crypt. And she was supposed to find something here among all the dead. Then she began to pray, every prayer she could think of. *Please God,* she thought, *don't let me end up like one of those bodies on the wall.*

FORTY-TWO

IT WASN'T BAD enough that Sapphire was missing the drugs. Now that teacher had to go missing. That hysterical skinny bitch was convinced that Sapphire had something to do with the kidnapping, but what possible connection could there be between the chaperone and the marijuana?

If someone was afraid that the chaperone might blab, how come they didn't go after the priest or the skinny bitch? They knew everything also. Unless the other chaperone had the drugs and was trying to make her own deal.

It didn't matter as long as they left Sapphire alone. In the meantime, there was only one thing that Sapphire could do. She would tell them about number 772. Whatever that was.

FORTY-THREE

SHE WAS FREEZING. She had to go the bathroom. She was starving. And she was scared out of her wits.

This is what nightmares are made of, she thought, kidnapped in a foreign country for no reason at all. *Stop feeling sorry for yourself,* she thought, *and just concentrate on a way out. I have to stall them as long as possible.* And then what? Who would ever find her here? They would kill her and bury her under one of the coffins. How perfect.

She wiped away her tears and forced herself to breathe deeply. She couldn't afford to be hysterical. Not now. Not when so much was at stake. It wouldn't do her any good to keep denying that she knew what they were talking about. They would kill her anyway and more quickly.

She lay there in the pit of darkness, with hot tears running down her face. And yet she kept repeating to herself, "I will not die. I will not die. I will not die." Maybe she could find a way out— maybe there was another exit that the men didn't know about. They hadn't tied her up—so she was relatively free.

So she began to walk, trying not to look to the right or the left—straight ahead. Except straight ahead was a little glass room so she had to turn around. On the left she got a glimpse of a body. The body of a woman.

At first it was difficult to see the woman—everything was a blur of panic and fear. Yet this woman didn't look like she had been lying there for a century, although she was wearing a nun's habit. But Mrs. Johnston could see wisps of highlighted hair. And there was a huge gash on her throat. But what really terrified her was that the woman only had one leg. And at the end of that one leg was one foot. And on that foot was a small golden ballet slipper.

And then Mrs. Johnston feared that it would only be a matter of time before she, too, would be there among all the corpses. Mrs. Johnston began to say all the prayers she had ever known and some that she didn't know and begged God to help her.

Then in the blackness she heard footsteps coming toward her. In the shadows a man dressed like a monk stood. His voice was hoarse, raspy, and strangely familiar. Could she have seen him in the cathedral? Was this the man in the confessional box who had scared Mrs. Hopwood? He looked horribly familiar, yet dreadfully altered. She was so confused.

"I must have fallen asleep," she said, "and I was having a bad dream."

"Well, your bad dream ain't over. Get up." He pointed a stubby forefinger at her, And then he kicked her. At any other point, Mrs. Johnston would be tempted to kick him right back but he might have a gun and she didn't know that he wouldn't kill her then and there. It was better to play scared, which wasn't hard to do.

She rose, staggered and fell down again. She was kicked a second time. She felt dizzy and weak. Fear bubbled in her stomach like acid. And then a horrible thought crossed her mind as the room swarmed before her. Maybe she was hallucinating—she had to be hallucinating. And in a few seconds the alarm clock would ring and it would be five forty-five—time to rise and head to St. Polycarp.

"Now, this is what is going to happen. In a few minutes my partner is going to come in here, and you're going to lead us to the merchandise."

"Okay," Mrs. Johnston gasped. "It's marijuana and it's in my suitcase. I left it in the car—well, you wouldn't let me take it. But it's all there. I swear it."

The front door slammed. She saw the kidnapper look at his watch with a puzzled expression on his face.

Maybe, Mrs. Johnston thought, maybe it was a guard, coming to close up. And maybe she was about to be saved. She tried to see the figure, but he was as blurry as an ink blot, finally emerging as a jittery shadow.

Better not scream, though, just in case. But it wouldn't hurt to talk. So she said in a very loud voice, "You don't have to worry. You won't have any trouble from me."

"We don't care about deodorant bottles full of marijuana. This is not what this is about."

Mrs. Johnston began to shake all over. If this wasn't about the drugs—then there was no hope. No hope at all.

"Either you know where the coin is or you don't. And if you don't, you are of no use to us."

Coin? What coin? Oh my God, what coin! She was trying to think of what to say. She could make something up and while they were searching for it, she could think of a plan—any plan. But instead, without even thinking, she said, "Please I have children, let me live." Hot tears streamed down her face.

"You've been overheard talking about that coin—so you have to know where it is."

"A coin?" Tears gushed from her eyes and she

gulped for air. "I swear I don't know anything about a coin."

"You were overheard saying it was a matter of life and death."

"Oh, that coin. No, no, no. You have misunderstood. I was talking about the penny that my little boy swallowed. You have to know all about that—it's how you lured me here. I mean, you have my phone, right?" She wanted to say more, to explain but her voice froze in her throat.

The man turned around and said to someone (surly he couldn't have been talking to the dead body but a shadow in the distance). "It's no use. Either she doesn't know, or she won't give it up."

And just like that all the pieces came together. A crime—Father Felix. He knew all about a stolen coin. The television. The missing woman Mrs. Hopwood kept blabbering about. Phoebe someone. Then she remembered the odd piece of paper she had seen on the plane—a paper which belonged to Father Felix. A body number—7, 2, *God, please help me to remember, please,* she prayed.

Why hadn't she thought of this before? Why had her terror prevented her from thinking clearly?

That man running from the confessional—the criminal. He must have stolen the coin. And hidden it. And Father Felix must know exactly where it was. This was what it was all about. 7—2—oh God, what was that other number?!

She opened her mouth but her tongue curled backward, making it impossible to speak. She managed to whisper, "I…"

And then she noticed it—in the dark—on the wall—what had just been a red blur was actually a fire alarm. All she had to do was pull it and help would be forthcoming. Why hadn't she seen that before?

She started to creep toward it and then she found herself crumpling to the floor. With blood thundering through her brain, the last sound she heard was the sound of gunfire, a bellowing explosion, and her head hit the cold hard concrete.

FORTY-FOUR

THEY DIDN'T BELIEVE HER. Father Felix could see that. But the way that Mrs. Hopwood was speaking so wildly, she did indeed appear delusional.

"Has she been drinking?" one of the detectives asked in Italian.

He shook his head. "It seems," Father Felix also spoke in Italian, "that one of our chaperones is missing. She flew home to be with her son. But according to her husband, nothing is wrong with her son."

"How do you know this?"

"She wrote Mrs. Hopwood a note saying her husband called."

"Then she lied?"

Father Felix grew mute.

"Maybe this woman—she doesn't like her life so much. She decide to run away to a little village."

"I suppose," Father Felix hesitated, "it is possible. She was always threatening such a thing."

"I've had enough!" Mrs. Hopwood leaped from the straight back chair where she had been sitting.

"What are you two saying? Whatever it is, I know it's not good. You don't look interested. You don't look concerned." She turned her fury to Father Felix. "Don't you care that one of your teachers has disappeared? This could be an international incident. I'm going to the papers."

"Sit down," the police officer said in perfect English.

Mrs. Hopwood, with a peevish look on her face, sank on the chair.

"A few days ago you came to us with a story about a missing handbag. And now it's a missing friend. Maybe your friend went to visit distant relatives in another part of Sicily and forgot to tell you."

"Mrs. Johnston is African-American. She does not have any distant relatives anyplace on this island."

"Is it possible that she just needed a few days away from her family and friends?" He turned towards Father Felix who lowered his eyes.

"No!" Mrs. Hopwood jerked upright again. "And if he told you such a thing then he is mistaken, badly mistaken! She wouldn't do that. And it's apparent that you're not going to follow this up."

"That's not true. We will certainly investigate

but you have to calm down." He turned away to answer a ringing phone. He was talking in Italian.

"What are they saying?" Mrs. Hopwood asked Father Felix. "Is it about Amelia?"

Father Felix was not about to tell her that they were talking about the missing coin. Instead he just shrugged.

"As I was saying—" the man swirled his chair around "—we will do everything in our power to find your friend but you must calm yourself."

"I will not calm myself until Mrs. Johnston is found," Mrs. Hopwood said scornfully. "And if I have to, I'll find her myself!"

"Ma'am, please, we're going to look for your friend. But try not to overreact. Now, how long has she been missing?"

"A little over a day," Father Felix said.

"That is not so long," the detective said in an airy manner. "Perhaps your friend decided to visit another part of Sicily and just forgot to tell you. Perhaps you had an argument of some sort and your friend merely needed some time to cool off. Sometimes when one is traveling, when one is on vacation, when one spends a lot of money—"

"We didn't spend any of our money," Mrs. Hopwood interrupted.

"The pressure to have a good time is overwhelming. And little spats can happen."

"No spat happened," Mrs. Hopwood practically spat the word. "And just so you know I'll do whatever I need to do to find my friend." And with that statement she marched out.

Father Felix had no choice but to follow her. Right to the hotel lobby where she stood in front of a bewildered clerk.

"My friend is missing," she started.

"Pardon, madam."

"My friend is missing. You know who I mean?"

"I do not."

Father Felix could tell that the clerk was becoming surly and had every right to do so because Mrs. Hopwood's manner was more than accusatory.

"She's a pretty black woman."

"Oh yes, I know exactly who you mean. She left here yesterday morning."

"Did her husband call her?"

"Pardon?"

"Are you having trouble understanding my English," Mrs. Hopwood demanded shrilly

"As a matter of fact, I am. Do you speak Italian?" he asked viciously.

"No, but he does." Mrs. Hopwood pushed Father Felix in front of her and demanded that he speak in Italian. "Ask him if he took the call from Peter."

"I'm sure that the police—"

"Ask him!" she shouted.

A group of tourists who had been reading over brochures while sitting on the hard plastic couches turned their attention to them. Well, at least they wouldn't understand what Father Felix was saying, not if he spoke Italian.

"Were you the one who talked to her husband? Yesterday, I mean."

He shook his head.

"Ask him who did," Mrs. Hopwood insisted.

"Do you know who did?"

He shook his head again but added, "I was the one who gave her the message. It was in her mailbox. It said her husband had called and there was something about her little boy swallowing something. She looked real upset. Then she went upstairs."

"What did he say?" Mrs. Hopwood asked anxiously.

Father Felix repeated the conversation. "Did he see her go?" Mrs. Hopwood nudged him.

Father Felix asked the clerk. "She came down about a half an hour later with a suitcase. She wanted me to call her a taxi."

"And did you?"

"Yes, I did. She said she would wait outside. A few minutes later I looked out the window and she was gone."

Father Felix had a real bad feeling in the pit of his stomach. Mrs. Johnston had obviously been duped. But for what reason? It wasn't as though someone was targeting tourists. They knew about her son. They waited outside, maybe even in a taxi. It was hard to believe that all of this had been caused by Sapphire and her drug smuggling. If that were the case, then why didn't the kidnappers snatch Mrs. Hopwood, who was clearly the more annoying of the two?

But there was little doubt Amelia Johnston was missing and she hadn't gone willingly. And how was he going to be able to return to the crypt with all this going on?

"What did he say?" Mrs. Hopwood screamed in his ear.

"He said she went upstairs and she packed and then she came down. He got her a taxi and she left."

"Is something wrong?" The clerk made the mistake of asking the question in English.

"You are darn right something is wrong!" Mrs. Hopwood bellowed. "My best friend has been kidnapped in your country. She's been gone for over twenty-four hours."

The tourists broke into a collective gasp.

"What happened?"

"How old was she?"

"Was it one of those motorcycle hoodlums?"

"Where did they get her?"

"Have you gone to the embassy?"

"The embassy," Mrs. Hopwood said thoughtfully. "We have to go to the embassy."

This was going to be a mess, Father Felix just knew it. Everyone was going to be talking about how they allowed a girl on their tour to smuggle in drugs and they might even believe that poor Mrs. Johnston was in on the drug plot.

And how on earth was he going to go to the crypt without drawing attention to himself? That was something he had to do before he left Sicily. But maybe he thought, as Mrs. Hopwood led him out of the hotel, maybe they wouldn't be leaving Sicily so soon after all.

FORTY-FIVE

HE COULDN'T BELIEVE that it was gone.

He had first thought that he had forgotten to lock his door. But then again the maid might have left it open. But it didn't matter because he hadn't really left anything in the room of value.

Or so he believed. He reached for his Bible—reading it always gave him comfort. And then he noticed that the scrap of paper where he had written the number was missing.

It must have fallen out, he reasoned. So he turned the book upside down, looking here and there—but nothing. The written number itself wasn't important—he had memorized it a long time ago. But the thought that someone had stolen it was disconcerting, especially with everything else that had happened.

Who else could have known about the coin and, more importantly, who else knew that *he* knew about the coin? He knelt down and said a prayer to St. Anthony—if it was just lost, the saint would come to the rescue. But Father Felix didn't know how well the saint worked with stolen items. He felt that it was all over now and Father Felix could not imagine how it all had gone so badly.

Maybe he was never meant to go to the crypt. Maybe it was God's way of telling him that he was breaking his priestly vows. Maybe he should just let it be—leave Sicily without knowing what was buried with those eight-thousand bodies. That would be the easy thing to do. But something deep inside of him said that this was wrong. And, at the very least, he had to try.

He wondered what had happened to Amelia Johnston. She was always threatening to leave home but no one took that seriously. As much as she complained about her life, he knew Mrs. Hopwood was right. Mrs. Johnston loved every minute of it. She adored her twins and her students and was attached to Julia Hopwood at the hip. For her to just vanish like that was totally out of character.

The police were questioning Sapphire, although he doubted if much would come of that. He couldn't imagine someone kidnapping Mrs. Johnston over a small amount of marijuana. Unless the drugs were just the tip of the iceberg.

But why take Amelia?

Anyway, there was nothing he could do now. Except pray. And make one last visit to the crypt.

He had a simple plan. He would go in as a tourist, late in the day. He knew exactly where the cameras were. He also knew the location of the janitor's closet. It would be a simple matter to hide while the monks were closing up. The coin was buried under body #772. He would hide a knife in his coat and it would be easy to cut a hole in the mesh. He would know one way or the other then. If he found the coin, then he would have a great deal to think about. But he didn't even want to consider that right now.

Never mind that, at the very least, he was breaking the law by defacing property. He'd find a way to prop the door open and then he would just leave. If worst came to worst, he would hide in the janitor's closet all night, and then just depart with the first tourists.

It sounded so simple. He looked out of his hotel window, which faced the street. The sun had gone down. The evening was gray and dismal, waiting for rain. Since they arrived in Sicily, it had been dark and gloomy.

The crypt closed at eight. It was seven o'clock now. Amelia Johnston had been missing for over a day. There was no benefit in thinking about that now. Tomorrow he would sort this all out. After he got through tonight. His resolve hardening, and feeling as if there were a fifteen-pound body bar on his shoulders, with leaden legs, he prepared for the long walk to the crypt.

FORTY-SIX

"I DON'T KNOW. I swear to you that I don't know." Sapphire was very close to crying. She couldn't believe that Mrs. Hopwood had actually called in the police.

"You understand you have broken international law." The fat policeman with the bushy brows loomed over her.

"I'm sure that Sapphire didn't mean for all of this to happen." Mrs. Hopwood was trying to be helpful but somehow Sapphire felt that with her interference, they were all going to land in a Sicilian jail.

Well, Mrs. Hopwood *should* land in a Sicilian jail with that priest, who was strangely absent. It was that heavyset woman who had caused all the problems by vanishing in the first place.

"Don't tell me what she means." The policeman turned his rage towards Mrs. Hopwood, who was teary-eyed herself. "You don't know what she means and it doesn't matter what she means. She broke the law. Besides, you are the one who insisted that what this young lady did caused the disappearance of your friend."

"It didn't." Sapphire could not resist the remark as she sprang from her chair.

"Sit down!" It was a female cop and she was even scarier than the other policeman. Her dark hair was pulled tightly in a bun. Her beady eyes were cold and unsympathetic. "Haven't you caused enough trouble?"

Sapphire sank down in the chair, a sense of hopelessness engulfing her. It was silent in the room. She could hear the small clock on the desk, ticking, marking time. Be tough, Sapphire told herself, be like steel. That's what she told herself each time her stepfather came toward her, when she heard her mother crying herself to sleep, when she saw the fear in her sister's eyes.

Be tough.

"I just think you should know something." Sapphire squared her shoulders and turned towards Mrs. Hopwood, who did indeed look rather curious.

"And what is that?" The policewoman had her hand on her thin hip.

"I found something in the alley."

"Yes?" Now the policewoman was just looking bored.

"A number."

"A phone number?" Mrs. Hopwood asked, although she looked rather suspicious.

"No, just a number. 772."

"So what," the policewoman fired at her.

"And then—" Sapphire was about to lie "—that priest, he dropped something."

"What priest?"

Mrs. Hopwood knew exactly what priest Sapphire was referring to. "The other chaperone."

"A piece of paper with that very same number written on it. Number 772."

"And this is important, why?" the policewoman demanded in an icy tone.

"I don't know exactly," Sapphire said stiffly. "But something awful is going on."

Mrs. Hopwood thought so, too. Sapphire could see by the way her sallow face paled.

"You're damn right something awful is going on," the police woman snapped. "And it doesn't have anything to do with number 772. It has to do with your drug trading."

"So what's going to happen now?" Mrs. Hopwood began to twist a disgusting piece of tissue.

"Now you said that this man called you again," the male cop asked.

"Yeah, he wasn't happy that I didn't show up. I had to make up some dumb excuse like I couldn't get out."

"Well, when you do show up, he really won't

be happy. Because we're going to set up a sting operation. If you cooperate—well, let me put it to you this way—if you don't cooperate, you won't be leaving our sunny country any time soon."

"There's nothing sunny about your country," Sapphire mumbled, even though she knew that insulting them wasn't smart.

"Will it be dangerous?" Mrs. Hopwood swallowed.

"Maybe," the woman cop snapped. "She should have thought of that before she agreed to be a carrier for a drug cartel."

"It wasn't a drug cartel," Sapphire protested, "and I only tried to do it once."

"I guess once was enough—" the male cop shrugged "—wasn't it?"

Sapphire couldn't think of anything clever to say. She was beaten and she knew it. If she ever wanted to get out of Sicily, she had to do exactly what she was told. God only knew what was going to happen once she got home. She had seen enough episodes of *Law & Order* to know that she was one dead duck. And all because that teacher had to go and disappear. She was the troublemaker. It was clear that Mrs. Hopwood wouldn't have said a solitary word. She was too scared. *I hope they never find her,* Sapphire thought, *I hope that she's gone for good.*

FORTY-SEVEN

Mrs. Hopwood sat in her hotel room, trying to make sense of this horrible nightmare.

Mrs. Johnston had vanished and there was no doubt in Mrs. Hopwood's mind that she hadn't left of her own accord, that she had been kidnapped.

Mrs. Hopwood tore the room apart, looking for some kind of clue but it was a useless endeavor. Mrs. Johnston had left no clue, of course, because she had no idea where she was going or why. Mrs. Hopwood reached inside the battered desk drawer and took out a piece of hotel stationery. Sometimes when she wrote things down, it was easier to sort things out.

So what did she know? Mrs. Johnston left thinking that Jeffrey was in the hospital and she was needed at home.

Who had made up such a story and left the message with the hotel clerk?

Why did they make up such a story?

How did they even know about Jeffrey to make up such a story? It came to her suddenly as she looked at her own useless cell phone lying on top of her suitcase. Mrs. Johnston had lost her cell phone. Or someone had stolen it. And that someone had never been Sapphire.

All that the person would have to do is look at calls received and listen to any message Amelia might have saved. And Amelia was always saving messages.

Now the question was why go to all that trouble. Mrs. Hopwood was convinced that Mrs. Johnston's disappearance had nothing to do with the drugs. It had to be something else.

Maybe—Mrs. Johnston had seen something, only she didn't realize it. Or maybe she knew something that she didn't even know she knew, but the kidnappers thought she did and would tell. It was like a bad movie on the mystery channel.

A stab of rage felt like a spike driven through her heart. But strangely enough it was not directed against the kidnappers, partially because they were faceless.

Her anger was directed, instead, straight at Father Felix. Where was he anyway? He hadn't even bothered to show up while she was being interrogated by those horrible policemen. He left her alone to deal with Sapphire and the awful mess that girl had created.

Everyone said that you never knew people until you traveled with them and that certainly turned out to be true in the case of Father Felix. The man who was a focused and dedicated principal turned out to be absolutely selfish and inflexible on vacation. Or maybe he wasn't selfish or inflexible. More like distracted. Both she and Mrs. Johnston had known that from the day they left. But right now Mrs. Hopwood's main concern was the missing Mrs. Johnston.

Except what if Father Felix's peculiar behavior had something to do with Mrs. Johnston's disappearance? It was unlikely, of course, but it might explain why he didn't seem to be the least bit concerned as to the whereabouts of Amelia. Because maybe he already knew. Maybe it all had to do with that confession, about the crime Father Felix was trying to solve. Maybe it had to do with the missing coin. And the missing criminal. And the missing Phoebe Medina. And that number—number 772.

But why take Amelia? Why not grab Father Felix? Unless they intended to use Mrs. Johnston as some kind of an elaborate pawn. She was still betting that Sapphire knew more than she was telling. So she set out to find her.

SAPPHIRE ANSWERED the door, looking irritated and exhausted. Mrs. Hopwood didn't wait for an invitation. She barged in.

"Sapphire, please, is there is anything you can tell me about Mrs. Johnston's disappearance—anything at all."

"I don't know anything about your friend. I told you that! Why don't you believe me?"

"Because I'm desperate." Mrs. Hopwood drew a deep breath. "Don't you think it's possible that Mrs. Johnston's disappearance has something to do with the drugs—that maybe someone kidnapped her?"

"Why would they?" Sapphire interrupted. "Why her? Why not me—or you?" Sapphire eyed Mrs. Hopwood. "Something tells me that you can be very annoying."

Mrs. Hopwood didn't bother to deny what was probably true. Instead she admitted that Mrs. Johnston had the drugs on her.

"Great," Sapphire said in a dull voice.

"So you see," Mrs. Hopwood said as her stomach fluttered, "that's the very reason they might go after her."

"Except how would they know such a thing?"

A despair washed over Mrs. Hopwood as she realized that Sapphire was right. How would the kidnappers have guessed that the drugs were in Mrs. Johnston's suitcase? And why not just take the suitcase?

Mrs. Hopwood hesitated before she asked the

next question. "Could there have been something in your diary?"

Sapphire's face reddened. "So you stole my diary!"

"I didn't…"

"But she did! Well, she got what she deserved. Where is it, my diary, I mean?"

Mrs. Hopwood shook her head.

"My diary had nothing to do with this!" Sapphire said enraged. "And I can't believe you broke into my room and stole my personal belongings, my drugs, my diary. Catholic school teachers are supposed to be above all that."

"We're only human," Mrs. Hopwood muttered.

"Yeah, well, let me tell you what I think, I think she just took off, you know, it happens. She had enough of you—and that horrible priest."

"She wouldn't do that. She wouldn't." Except Mrs. Hopwood wished that it was a possibility.

"Why don't you ask him? The priest, I mean."

Again Mrs. Hopwood shook her head.

"Get out!" Sapphire flung the door open. "Fine chaperones you turned out to be. I don't trust any one of you. And, if you had a brain in your head, you wouldn't trust anyone, either."

MRS. HOPWOOD HEADED for her room. She had to admit that Sapphire might have a point. Father

Felix knew more than he was telling. And Mrs. Hopwood would have to speak to him immediately.

Just in case there was danger, she grabbed her high-heel shoe and inserted the small ice pick she had bought. It fit perfectly.

Then she stumbled down the long, winding hall, found Father Felix's door and rapped loudly. Nothing. Where could he be?

"He's not there." An obese busboy wheeling a cart of leftover food bolted down the narrow corridor.

"I suppose you don't know where he's gone," Mrs. Hopwood mumbled.

"Well, he did ask me for directions. A shortcut to the crypt."

Mrs. Hopwood immediately perked up. "The crypt? We already went to the crypt."

The busboy merely shrugged and continued pushing the tray down the hallway. Mrs. Hopwood followed him. "Are you sure it was today?" she asked.

"Pardon?"

"When did he ask you this?" She spoke slowly and deliberately.

The busboy seemed annoyed by her questions and actually sneered at Mrs. Hopwood. "Just now." He jabbed at the elevator button.

Just now. Father Felix had gone to the crypt. Just now. Something was up. Mrs. Hopwood could do nothing about Mrs. Johnston's disappearance.

"Could you tell me the shortcut?"

In broken English the busboy repeated streets, none of which Mrs. Hopwood could understand. Then he frowned at her, when he noticed that she didn't have her handbag with her.

"I'll catch you next time," she mumbled a lie.

The elevator snapped open. Maybe if she ran into the street, she could catch Father Felix and confront him.

She rode down with the sullen busboy, ran through the lobby and into the street. In the distance, she could see a lone man, heading down the darkened road. Abandoning caution, she hurried to follow him.

FORTY-EIGHT

SAPPHIRE COULD NOT believe that she was going to do this—a sting. But what choice did she have? The number 772 proved to be utterly useless.

So when the man called again for the third time and demanded the drugs, actually threatening her, she agreed to meet him in the alley. But she was terrified. What if? What if the man became enraged when he realized that she didn't have the drugs and slit her throat before the police could come? What if the man suspected he had been set up and stabbed her in the heart before the police could come? What if the police were incompetent and never did come? What if the police were corrupt and they had set her up to be murdered because she knew too much and had failed them and exposed the operation?

What if?

What if?

What if she was doomed and this had been her fate all along?

"DON'T WORRY," they told her, "we're on the other side of the alley."

They gave her a wire and ran it down her T-shirt.

It was lumpy and Sapphire was convinced it was noticeable.

"Not in the dark," they told her.

"Not unless he touches me," she retaliated.

"Then don't let him." The policewoman, who looked like the Grim Reaper, stared at her with those coal-black eyes. "Just remember you have to get him to ask for the drugs—to show you the money—to admit to the crime. As soon as he does that, we'll be on the scene."

"But what if he doesn't—" Sapphire worried "—what if something goes wrong?"

"We'll be on the scene," the cop promised.

They handed her a bag full of deodorant bottles—deodorant bottles, which contained nothing but deodorant.

"What if he looks into them and finds out they're empty?" Sapphire asked.

"We'll be on the scene," the cop repeated.

But Sapphire had heard a lot of promises and almost all of them had been broken. There was no reason to believe that this was different. Like every other time in her life, however, she had no choice.

She waited, with trembling legs, her heart thumping, praying under her breath.

Why had her chaperones been so smart? Why couldn't they have been stupid?

The more she thought about it, the angrier she

became. She was a good person. She knew she was a good person. Life had been so unfair to her, and then to die this way, so far away from home—when all she wanted to do was protect her sister—it just wasn't right.

Who had ever protected her? And the more she thought about it, the angrier she became. And the less afraid.

She heard movement behind her. She whipped around.

A young, skinny kid stood in the alley. Sapphire couldn't believe that this was her contact. He looked more frightened than she was.

"You got the stuff?" he asked in a thick Italian accent.

"Here." She showed him the tote bag.

"Hand it over." He was trying to sound audacious but Sapphire had a lifetime, pretending to be audacious herself.

"Not until I see the money. American money," she added. "I don't want to deal with a foreign bank."

The skinny kid reached in his pocket and took out a wad of bills. "Five hundred dollars in twenties. So where's the stuff?"

For one crazy moment Sapphire thought about taking the money and running—she could outrun the kid and maybe the cops. But sooner or later they would catch her. That was just the way it was.

A loud, blaring sound filled the air. The skinny kid's eyes widened with terror as they were surrounded.

"You set me up." He spit on the ground.

"Yeah, I guess I did." She actually felt bad for him, for herself, as well. Because then she walked right alongside of him—in handcuffs.

FORTY-NINE

HIS HEART WAS beating at an abnormal rate as he walked down the narrow halls of the crypt, trying to pretend that he was just another tourist, horrified by the sights in front of him. Not that he was a man who was about to steal something from one of the bodies. Body #772.

It didn't look any different than any other body. Just another poor soul, lying down on a coffin. Except for the large gray hook dangling from one of the arms.

Was the coin somewhere on the body or was this just a wild goose chase? When he thought about what he was about to do, shivers ran down his spine. Don't think about it, he told himself, just do it.

He walked around, hoping he was inconspicuous in his khakis and his short-sleeved shirt (except maybe he should have brought a cardigan. It was quite cold in here probably to keep the bodies fresh, so to speak). He didn't wear a collar. A collar would tell everyone that he was a priest.

A collar would be noticed. He couldn't afford to be noticed.

He watched a group of tourists, a family of French foreigners, a husband, a wife and two teenage girls, who were taking great delight as they viewed the dilapidated bodies, then a single woman, walking around with a brochure and two men who were peering into the screens as though they were looking for something in particular. The gold coin? And then a whole flock of Americans, discussing where they should go for dinner. Father Felix would have given anything to be part of that group.

When he thought that no one was looking, he slipped around the corner, away from the video camera, found the janitor's closet and closed the door behind him.

What if someone saw him? What would he say? That he was feeling faint and he needed to be away from the crowd—he was looking for a bathroom? The truth was that he was feeling rather faint—faint and sick.

He sat down on the floor and closed his eyes, leaning against the floorboard. He decided to say the rosary, just to pass the time and because he felt that maybe he should be praying. He would pray that he was doing the right thing. And then he would pray that if he wasn't doing the right thing, God would forgive him anyway.

He heard the announcement in Italian, in French, in English and finally in Spanish. The crypt was closing in seven minutes. Everyone needed to leave. As the voices faded away, he continued to pray. And then the lights went out.

He didn't move. He didn't dare move. Even though he was freezing cold and the sweat was pouring down his face. He had thought about this so many times. It was hard to believe that he was actually doing it.

Okay, he thought, between Hail Marys, what is the worst thing that can happen? I can get arrested for breaking and entering. Except he really wasn't breaking in. He had already been in. And although he was about to steal something, no one knew exactly what he was after. And besides, he was only going to return the item to its rightful owner.

He waited and waited and he guessed about a half an hour had passed. Then he slowly opened the door and peered out. There wasn't a living soul in sight. He walked down the hall and noticed an exit door. He should leave it open—so he could quickly leave.

He hoped there wasn't going to be an alarm. There wasn't. But the door wouldn't stay open—

silly to think it would. He looked around for something to hold it ajar but could find nothing. The crypt wasn't exactly full of useful items. So he took off one of his shoes and used it to prop open the door.

And then he began walking with one shoe—through the soldier's section, and the virgin's section, and then on to the professional section—where he stopped abruptly.

A nun was lying there with a look of horror and shock on her face. What made Father Felix stop and stare was that he recognized the habit—the Sisters of St. Joseph—a habit that was designed only last year. While he was thinking of what this all might mean, he heard creaking and the ominous sound of footsteps.

FIFTY

WAS SHE CRAZY? Where did Mrs. Hopwood think she was going? She had no umbrella and it certainly looked like rain. What she should do—the sensible thing to do was to turn around and go right back to the hotel. And she was wearing those horrible heels. What possessed her to always be wearing the wrong shoes? Sure they were pretty, but half the time no one noticed and the people who did, either thought she was insane to allow herself to be so uncomfortable—or that she was lame.

If I ever get back to the States, she thought, I'll never wear high heels again. I'll give them all to Goodwill or better yet, I'll throw them all down in the incinerator. She stared down at her shoes and was tempted to take them off and walk barefoot. The size of the heel had to be at least four inches. Well, maybe, just maybe that ice pick would come in handy. It gave her some consolation as she followed the black figure in front of her.

With each step she knew that what she was doing was insane. She should be back in the hotel and phoning the police. Like that did a lot of good last time. But Amelia Johnston had been her best friend for many years and Mrs. Hopwood really believed that if the situation was reversed Amelia would do the same for her. How could Mrs. Hopwood just leave Sicily—not knowing where friend was or why she disappeared?

Maybe as time passed the Sicilian police would take more of an interest. But as time passed, Mrs. Hopwood also knew, her chances of finding her friend alive would diminish. She could leave it in Father Felix's hands, but she didn't feel good about that. Not at all. Even Mrs. Johnston agreed that Father Felix had acted peculiarly from the first day of this trip (actually it was he who had arranged the trip). There was little doubt now in Mrs. Hopwood's mind that he had something to do with Mrs. Johnston's disappearance. And maybe Mrs. Johnston was right two years ago. Maybe Father Felix wasn't a serial killer—but maybe he wasn't a priest, either.

And there was something about that number—772. Mrs. Hopwood was guessing something was hidden beneath that body and that's what Father Felix was after. Maybe the coin everyone was talking about. The truth was that she didn't care what he was after—as long as it didn't involve Mrs. Johnston. Maybe she could blackmail him.

Maybe that's what Mrs. Johnston did and maybe that's why she went missing. Maybe Mrs. Hopwood should go home. Instead she hurried to follow the man they had called Father through the streets.

MUCH TO HER SURPRISE when she arrived at the crypt, she found a side door ajar. And it was also being propped open with a shoe which she recognized as belonging to Father Felix. She found this comforting. Father Felix was inside. He could protect her. But didn't she just admit to herself that he might be a killer or, at the very least, an imposter? But then again, if she could get in so easily—then she could also get out. She opened the door just a shade wider and sneaked in. But she had dislodged the black loafer and the door slammed behind her. This was not good. Not good at all.

FIFTY-ONE

HE HEARD THE DOOR close and he doubted that it was the wind. Someone else was in the crypt and now what was he to do? He was a priest, after all, first and foremost. And he wasn't afraid, Well, not really. So he drew a deep breath and came out of hiding. He stood in the blackened aisle, careful not to look at the corpses on either side of him or above him, where they paraded. One child was actually pushing a baby carriage with the skeleton of a newborn. This is a bad dream, he thought, and in a moment I will wake up in the rectory. He heard crying.

"Is anyone there?"

"It's me, Mrs. Hopwood." Her voice came from a distance.

"What are you doing here?" He walked towards her. She was standing in full view of the camera, wearing a polka-dot dress with spike heels. For a moment, he thought he was hallucinating.

"I need to know what's going on and something tells me you know exactly where Amelia is."

"I swear to you…"

"Look, I know all about number seven hundred and seventy-two and I know that you're looking for something hidden there, probably that coin."

Father Felix was stunned and found himself stammering. "How—how—"

"It doesn't matter how, and it's too hard to explain now. I don't want any part of it. I just need to know what happened to Amelia."

"What are you talking about? I don't know anything. If I…"

Mrs. Hopwood began to wrinkle her nose. "Do you smell it?"

"The dead don't smell, although God knows they should."

"No—it's that honeysuckle."

Suddenly there were footsteps. He found himself edging towards Mrs. Hopwood, who was edging away from him, almost in fear.

We've been caught, he thought, and actually that's not a bad thing. I should never have come here—this whole thing is insane—what was I thinking?

He heard Mrs. Hopwood gasp.

"Oh my God, Judy, are we glad to see you! How did you find us? You would not believe what happened!"

And just as Mrs. Hopwood was about to go into

great detail, Father Felix asked, "Why are your hands behind your back?"

And then Father Felix noticed something he hadn't noticed before. There was something about Judy's eyes—something that wasn't right. Her brown eye was pointing one way, her blue eye the other. And while Father Felix was wondering if perhaps it wasn't just a trick of the light, Judy whipped out a small pistol.

"It's you," Father Felix whispered in disbelief, "you were the one who stole that coin?"

"I guess you could say that. Only I didn't do it alone. There were four of us. Just like the painting of the angels except one of us was a traitor. That stupid fool confessed. And he confessed to you. Then he actually told us about it. He was a coin collector and he was supposed to sell it. Then he had second thoughts. We wondered how long it would be before you flew to Sicily and tried to get the coin for yourself. And we have been following you ever since."

"No," he stuttered. "You got it all wrong, I just wanted…" He looked up at the cameras. Now they were all standing in the middle of the hall. Maybe someone was monitoring them from afar and later on—when he and Mrs. Hopwood were dead and buried—would be, too.

Judy caught on right away. "Don't bother looking there," she spat. "The cameras were disabled months ago."

"You killed that woman, didn't you?" Father Felix asked. "That Phoebe Medina."

Mrs. Hopwood was making strange mewing noises, almost like a cat and staring in the distance.

"Not me. But let's just say that she had an accident," Judy said in a dismissive voice. "Her husband was the coin collector. After he confessed to you and died…"

"Her husband died?" Father Felix asked breathlessly.

"Yeah, he died. Had a heart attack. I guess confessing was too much for him. Of course, if you had known that before…"

"If I had known that before…" Father Felix echoed.

"Then you wouldn't have been compelled to keep the seal of confession, now would you? You see, I was raised Catholic."

"Well, if you were raised Catholic…"

Father Felix was tempted to go into one of his lengthy sermons about doing the right thing, but it was probably much too late for that. Besides, even Father Felix knew that his sermons weren't particularly convincing.

He needn't have worried. Judy didn't give him a

chance. "That wife actually thought she was going to get her share. The curator of the museum was so stupid, he killed her without finding out where the coin was hidden. And, of course, it wouldn't have been possible without the security guard here, who incidentally is my boyfriend."

"The security guard?" Father Felix couldn't believe what he was hearing. "But he's a monk!"

Judy laughed and it echoed through the empty corridor.

"But why take Mrs. Johnston?" Father Felix asked as he tried to reach for the knife in his pocket.

"Because she was the easiest to get alone and when I heard her talking about a coin, I thought she might know something."

"Listen, if it's the coin you're after, you can have it," Mrs. Hopwood said suddenly. "It's all yours. I would say you earned it. And I know where it is. Just let Mrs. Johnston go and we'll forget all about this."

"She's dead."

Father Felix felt his legs shaking "I don't understand," he stumbled.

"What is there to understand?" Judy said roughly. "She's dead."

"Amelia," he gasped, "dead?" He felt as though he needed to sit down but there was no chair in sight. Instead he slid down on the cold, hard floor. The knife slipped out of his hand, and clattered on the floor, useless against the steadied pistol. "Can you at least take us to her so I can administer last rites?"

"I'd be happy to take you to her. Well, maybe happy isn't the right word. But I *will* take you to her. After you take me to the coin."

"Amelia, dead." Try as she might, Father Felix could not grasp the enormity of it all. "I didn't mean for any of this to happen. Never. No coin is worth Mrs. Johnston's life."

"Just take me to the damn coin," Judy demanded. She pointed the pistol at him and reached on the floor for his knife.

"It's under the body—number 772. I think it's in this direction."

He felt as though he was sleepwalking as he led the way and Mrs. Hopwood fell in behind him and Judy behind them both. It occurred to him that now that Judy had admitted that she was a thief and a murderer she had nothing to lose and she was going to shoot him and Mrs. Hopwood in the back. Mrs. Hopwood must have had the same thought because she was making a poor attempt to recite the Act of Contrition.

They stopped in front of a man who had died long ago and seemed to be sleeping peacefully.

Judy took his knife in one hand, still pointing the pistol ferociously in the other, and she cut into the screen. She dragged the body out, where it disintegrated on the floor, the flesh peeling off like tissue paper.

"It's not here," Judy whispered in shock, "it's not here."

"It has to be. I was told that number. I know I was." Father Felix was having a hard time believing it himself. "Unless someone got here first."

"Shut up!"

Judy was bent over the body, tearing it apart. She had dropped the knife beside the man's left arm, which had become detached from the torso.

While Father Felix was wondering if he should grab for the knife, he saw Mrs. Hopwood fumbling with her shoes. Father Felix released a frustrated gasp. Mrs. Hopwood was about to die and her first and last concern was for her shoe.

Her heel had fallen off. Well, she probably wouldn't be walking again. Ever. While Judy reached for the gun, Father Felix saw something long and sharp in Mrs. Hopwood's hand.

It happened so fast—he could scarcely comprehend it. One moment Mrs. Hopwood was holding a sharp, pointed steel object. The next moment the sharp pointed, steel object was in the back of Judy's neck.

Judy gave a gurgle and collapsed, dropping the gun.

"We have to find Amelia," Mrs. Hopwood said.

"There's a thousand bodies here," Father Felix's voice echoed. "She could be anywhere."

"I don't believe she's dead," Mrs. Hopwood repeated, "I don't believe she's dead. I would know if she was dead."

"Help me," Judy's voice came up raspy. "Please help me."

Father Felix stood paralyzed.

"Pick up the gun," Mrs. Hopwood screamed.

Father Felix stared at her.

"I don't like guns," she said. "They're dangerous."

He lifted the gun. It was cold and heavy. He had never held a gun before and he wasn't sure where to point it, so he aimed for the floor—and wondered if he should be administering last rites to Judy.

"Forget about us helping you. Not until you tell us what you did with Amelia Johnston," Mrs. Hopwood demanded.

"She's in the embalming room—at the end of the hall."

"Maybe I should give Judy last rites." Father Felix was feeling faint and confused. "She seems to be choking on her blood."

"The hell with that. What about Mrs. Johnston? Doesn't she deserve last rites?"

"Judy might need them more."

"Am I dying?" Judy whispered.

"You're going straight to hell," Mrs. Hopwood said viciously.

Mrs. Hopwood grabbed the knife on the floor. But the knife caught on the dead man and turned him over one more time.

Something clanged.

"It's the coin," Mrs. Hopwood said. "It fell out of his eye. Yuck! I'm not touching it."

Father Felix had no qualms. He reached for the coin and tucked it away.

And then he saw Mrs. Hopwood running to the far side of the wall. She pressed down and the deafening sound of a fire alarm blared through the building.

FIFTY-TWO

MRS. JOHNSTON FELT the cold, hard floor beneath her head. She tried to remember what had happened. Someone shot her and she fell. Her entire body ached. She heard voices and scurrying footsteps. She could swear that Father Felix and Mrs. Hopwood were close by. She was already dead. She must be. Was this hell? Where was the fire—the devils—the angels? Where was God?

"I know this is the way. I've been here before."

"When?"

"When you were hiding on me—you know—the first time we visited the crypt."

"I wasn't hiding on you. I just didn't want you to get involved. I didn't want anyone to get hurt."

"Too late for that."

Maybe that's what it meant to be dead. You heard everything around you but you couldn't do anything, or say anything. Should all this pain be blazing through her?

The door burst open and in walked Mrs. Hopwood, wearing one red shoe. And Father Felix was holding a gun.

Mrs. Johnston released a shrill scream and she was startled by the sound of her own voice.

"It's me, Amelia! Julia!" Mrs. Hopwood limped over and knelt down by her side. "Look, she's alive!"

"I'm dead. I must be dead. She shot me. The tour guide."

Mrs. Hopwood looked down at the fanny pack. "There's a bullet hole here." She unzipped it. "Look, the bullet was stopped by your medal of St. Rosalia."

"Guess she saved my life." Mrs. Johnston closed her eyes as Mrs. Hopwood shook her desperately. "Don't die, don't die."

"I'm not going to die. I want to go home."

"So do I," Mrs. Hopwood agreed. "So do I."

FIFTY-THREE

MRS. JOHNSTON was promptly escorted to a hospital to be checked over and Mrs. Hopwood had a choice to either accompany her friend or to go to the police station with Father Felix. Mrs. Johnston seemed as right as rain, although she was angry and ungrateful. After all, Mrs. Hopwood had clearly saved her life and risked her own in the process. So Mrs. Hopwood chose the police station, which seemed to her to be a more interesting choice because she had already heard what happened to Mrs. Johnston again—and again.

It was not.

She should have realized that—because Father Felix spoke in Italian and was answered in Italian. She had to ask what was being said, but they were impatient the few times they answered her. Didn't anyone realize that she was clearly the hero? If it wasn't for her, Judy would be gone with the coin, instead of being arrested and trying to make a deal by ratting on her friends. And they would all be dead.

From what Mrs. Hopwood could discern, Father Felix told them that four people had robbed the coin. One man took the coin and, fearing that the police were after him, and, at the suggestion of the security guard of the crypt, he hid the coin under one of the bodies in the crypts. The other three, which included Judy, the curator at the museum and the guard at the crypt, had no idea which body the coin was under. Although the security guard had done a lot of searching, he had come up empty-handed.

Then because his father was dying in the United States, the robber left suddenly. While in the States, his conscience bothered him and he decided to confess to Father Felix.

"It's all over." Father Felix pushed her into a cab. "Tomorrow we go home and we can forget all about this. I did my duty. The coin has been returned, and Judy and her cohorts will be arrested."

"Thanks to me," Mrs. Hopwood muttered and then she asked thoughtfully. "I wonder how Mrs. Johnston made out."

"She made out just fine," Father Felix said, "and don't go causing troubles when there are none."

Mrs. Hopwood didn't say what she was thinking. In all the years she had known Mrs. Johnston she was never fine. And Mrs. Hopwood doubted very much if she would be now.

FIFTY-FOUR

"SO WHAT ARE WE going to do with the reward money," Mrs. Hopwood asked as she sipped her cappuccino and took a last look at Sicily.

"How do you get to we?" Mrs. Johnston stuffed a cassata in her mouth. "I was the one who was kidnapped and shot."

"It seems to me," Father Felix stirred his cappuccino, "that the money really belongs to me. If it wasn't for that man confessing and my determination to set things right…"

"If it wasn't for me and my ice pick, none of this would matter in the least—" Mrs. Hopwood eyed the almond cookies "—we'd all be dead."

"I don't care." Mrs. Johnston grabbed the cookie. "I was the one who was injured. And besides—" she turned toward Father Felix "—didn't you take a vow of poverty?"

"I didn't take a vow of poverty," Mrs. Hopwood said quickly.

"You didn't take any vows at all." Mrs. Johnston chewed the cookie.

"If we split it three ways," Mrs. Hopwood said hopefully.

"We have to put the money aside." Father Felix grimaced as he took a sip of his espresso. "We have no idea of what's coming around the bend. Some of the girls are complaining and who knows—their parents may decide to sue us for putting them in a dangerous position—on the trail of that stolen coin."

"Well, by your own admission—" Mrs. Johnston was eying the chocolate cupcake "—the whole thing was your idea."

"By the way—" Father Felix turned towards Mrs. Hopwood "—how did you know where the coin was buried?"

"Sapphire told the police."

"The police," Father Felix and Mrs. Johnston said in unison.

"They didn't pay her any mind," Mrs. Hopwood said breezily. "They didn't understand the significance of the number and neither did she."

"But how did she find out," Father Felix wondered.

"She said you dropped the paper."

"I didn't drop it. She stole it."

"So she's a thief and a drug dealer," Mrs. Johnston said with some degree of satisfaction. "Of course, once I read her diary—well, she has a very bad life."

"You're talking about being a thief?" Mrs. Hopwood stuffed another cookie in her mouth. "You should give that diary back to her."

"I already did," Mrs. Johnston said. "And she was hardly grateful."

"I feel a little sorry for her," Father Felix said. "They're sending her back to the States with us and letting the legal system there sort it out. She has had a pretty rough time of it and her home life will be taken into consideration. Abusive stepfather, alcoholic mother. They're going to put her sister into a foster home—if they can find one." His eyes bore straight into Mrs. Hopwood's.

"Oh no, don't even look my way, I already have one rebellious teenager."

"Who is going to college in the fall," Father Felix reminded her. "And you will have that spare room."

"Are you both crazy?" Mrs. Hopwood managed to point at Mrs. Johnston, who could not protest since her mouth was full of cream. "What about her? Sapphire and her sister would be a tremendous help with those two rambunctious twins."

"No way," Mrs. Johnston, "I hate teenagers."

"But you teach them," Mrs. Hopwood said.

"Which is why I hate them."

"Just a thought," Father Felix shrugged.

"Would you please keep your thoughts to yourself," Mrs. Hopwood suggested, not too kindly.

Father Felix ignored her and then said, "You know how the church has been leaning to one side and it's built under that fault. And the parishioners are terrified that it's going to collapse during one of my sermons. Perhaps it's time to level it."

"That ground hasn't been dug up for two-hundred years," Mrs. Hopwood said. "God only knows what's beneath that earth."

"Yes," Mrs. Johnston said. "God only knows."

* * * * *

REQUEST YOUR FREE BOOKS!

2 FREE NOVELS
PLUS 2 FREE GIFTS!

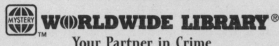

WORLDWIDE LIBRARY®
Your Partner in Crime

God's Holy Presence

Thou hast made us for
Thyself, and the heart of
man is restless until
it finds its rest in thee.
St. Augustine

Be strong and courageous!
For the Lord your God is with
you wherever you go. JOSHUA
1:9

Where two or three gather
together as my followers,
I am there among them
Matthew 18:20

Wait
upon GOD and feel His good Presence, this will carry you
evenly through your days
business: William Penn The
Lord your GOD is living among
you. He is a mighty SAVIOR.
ZephANiAH 3:17

CONSCIENCE is God's Presence
in man. Emanuel SWEDENBORG.
Come CLose to God and God will
come close to you. James 4:8

I feel something of that hidden but
Powerfull presence of Christ